PUFFIN BOOKS

THE ROPE AND OTHER STORIES

Philippa Pearce is the daughter of a miller and grew up in a mill-house near Cambridge. The house, the river and the village feature in many of her best-loved children's books. She was educated at the Perse Girls' School in Cambridge and then at Girton College, Cambridge, where she read English and history. In addition to writing a great many books, she has also worked as a scriptwriter-producer for the BBC, a children's book editor, a book reviewer, a lecturer, a storyteller and as a freelance writer for radio and newspapers. Her now classic books in Puffin include Carnegie Medal winner *Tom's Midnight Garden*, *What the Neighbours Did*, *A Dog So Small* and *The Battle of Bubble and Squeak*, which won the Whitbread Award. Philippa Pearce lives in Cambridgeshire.

# PHILIPPA PEARCE

# the rope and other stories

Illustrated by Annabel Large

PUFFIN BOOKS

PUFFIN BOOKS

Published by the Penguin Group
Penguin Books Ltd, 80 Strand, London WC2R 0RL, England
Penguin Putnam Inc., 375 Hudson Street, New York, New York 10014, USA
Penguin Books Australia Ltd, 250 Camberwell Road, Camberwell, Victoria 3124, Australia
Penguin Books Canada Ltd, 10 Alcorn Avenue, Toronto, Ontario, Canada M4V 3B2
Penguin Books India (P) Ltd, 11 Community Centre, Panchsheel Park, New Delhi – 110 017, India
Penguin Books (NZ) Ltd, Cnr Rosedale and Airborne Roads, Albany, Auckland, New Zealand
Penguin Books (South Africa) (Pty) Ltd, 24 Sturdee Avenue, Rosebank 2196, South Africa

Penguin Books Ltd, Registered Offices: 80 Strand, London WC2R 0RL, England

www.penguin.com

'Bluebag' first published under the title 'The Nest' in
*Cricket*, vol. 3, no. 2, August 1976
'Inside her Head' first published in *Puffin Post*, vol. 14, no. 3, in 1980
'The Rope' first published in *The Fiction Magazine*, vol. 5, no. 5, July 1986
'The Nest Egg' first published in *Once Upon a Planet*, an anthology of stories and extracts in aid
of Friends of the Earth, published by Puffin Books, 1989

This collection published 2000
5

Text copyright © Philippa Pearce, 1976, 1980, 1986, 1989, 2000
Illustrations copyright © Annabel Large, 2000
All rights reserved

The moral right of the author and illustrator has been asserted

Set in 13/16 Bembo
Typeset by Rowland Phototypesetting Ltd,
Bury St Edmunds, Suffolk

Made and printed in England by Clays Ltd, St Ives plc

British Library Cataloguing in·Publication Data
A CIP catalogue record for this book is available from the British Library .

ISBN 0–141–30914–8

# Contents

# The Rope

The rope hung from top to bottom of his dream. The rope hung softly, saying nothing, doing nothing. Then the rope began to swing very softly, very gently, at first only by a hair's breadth from the vertical . . . Towards him.

Mike could not see the swing of it, but he knew that it was happening.

The rope swung a little wider, a little wider . . . Towards him.

The rope had no noose at the end of it, but Mike knew it was a hangman's rope, as surely as if the rope had told him so; and he knew it was for him.

The rope swung a little wider, a lot wider . . .

1

Wide, wide it swung . . . Towards him, towards him . . .

Mike shrieked and woke himself, and found that he had only squeaked, after all. He had woken nobody, for he was sleeping alone, downstairs, on the couch in his granny's sitting-room. That was because Shirley and his mother were occupying the spare room upstairs; and, of course, Gran herself was in her own bedroom.

Thankfully he lay awake, but gradually thankfulness left him. He got out of his couch-bed, went to the window and drew back the curtains to look out at the early morning weather.

Please, please, let there be rain . . . or at least a heavy sky that promised – that faithfully promised – rain later.

But the sky was blue and cloudless, and there was sunshine already in Gran's little garden, and sunshine on the meadow beyond and on the trees that grew along the river-bank. The river bounded the meadow, and on the far bank several very tall trees grew. One of them was Mike's gallows, his gibbet.

He got back into bed. He didn't sleep again – he didn't want to. He didn't want the morning's happenings to begin earlier than need be. He dozed, until he had to get up because everybody else was up and about.

At breakfast Shirley said, 'Can we go to the rope this morning?'

'Of course,' said their grandmother. 'You can both

swim well, can't you? If necessary, that is. When I was your age —'

It always seemed that Gran had been a bit of a tomboy at their age: a *successful* tomboy. You could see that Shirley liked to think she resembled her granny in this. Perhaps, thought Mike, she really did.

Their mother — Gran's daughter-in-law, not her daughter — said uneasily, 'We're here on such a short visit; and there are other places to go to besides the river and that rope . . .' The river was not deep or fast-flowing, or even very wide; but it was certainly very muddy. 'If either of them fell in . . .'

Their gran said, 'Nonsense! What's a little river-water in summer to them, at their age?'

So, altogether, it had to be taken for granted that they would go to the river, to the rope.

And it certainly wasn't going to rain this morning; but oh! Mike thought, it just possibly could in the afternoon. So he must manoeuvre and contrive. He said, 'We can go to the river this morning and to Brown's this afternoon. I expect there'll still be a few comics left.' Brown's was the newsagent's in the village.

'*Left?*' said Shirley. 'A few comics *left*?'

'They go very quickly,' said Mike.

'Oh!' said Shirley. Then: 'No, let's do Brown's this morning; the rope this afternoon.'

'If you say so,' said Mike. He also shrugged his shoulders.

Their grandmother had given them money to buy comics – enough money to buy at least one each. When they reached Brown's, Shirley was business-like in her examining and choosing; Mike mooned around, flipping pages, dissatisfied. Here, in this one, was the kind of story he usually enjoyed. Mighty-righty – that was the hero's name – was tough and fearless. He also had magic powers. In an emergency, he just pressed a button on his chest and little luminous wings sprouted from his shoulders to carry him any-where. (The wings could be retracted by the same device.) Moreover, if he clenched his right hand once, it became a fist to knock out a champion boxer; twice, and he could knock down trees and walls. (It was pos-sible that he could clench it a third time and so acquire even superior power; but that was only hinted at in the story.)

'I saw you yesterday,' said a voice at Mike's elbow. 'Yesterday evening. By the river.' A ginger-haired boy of about Mike's age; he sounded friendly.

'Oh,' said Mike.

'Have you come to live in one of those houses beyond the meadow?'

'No,' said Mike. 'Only staying. With our gran. Two days.'

'Have you seen the rope?' asked the ginger-haired boy.

'Yes,' said Mike.

'We're going there later,' said Shirley eagerly.

4

'See you then,' said the ginger-haired boy. He left the shop with a packet of sweets that he had just bought.

Mike put Mighty-righty back on the display-shelf. 'I don't want any of them,' he said. 'They're rubbish.'

Shirley, not really expecting any luck, asked if she could use Mike's share of the money they had been given; and, to her amazement, he said that she could. He was very quiet as they walked back from Brown's; but Shirley was dipping into her comics as she went, and noticed nothing. He was silent over their mid-day meal with the others; but no one noticed because Gran was hurrying everything today. She wanted the children to have plenty of time by the river, with the rope.

Mike offered to stay and help with the washing-up, but his granny told him that she and his mother would do it. He must go off with his sister – no time like the present, for their age. So Mike and Shirley went alone across the meadow, in blazing sunshine, to the river and the trees on the river-bank.

There it hung: the rope.

A tall tree leaned over the river, and one end of the rope had been attached to a high branch of it, so that the rope hung down over the river. It hung to within a hand's breadth of the surface of the water, almost exactly over the middle of the river.

That was how it had hung yesterday evening, when Mike and Shirley had first seen it; but already today someone had waded or swum out to the rope and caught the end of it and brought it back to the far bank – the far bank, as far as Mike and Shirley were concerned. They looked across and saw the boy who must have taken the rope in this way. He was dripping with river-water and shivering; and, at the same time, he was laughing and talking with the friends gathered round him. Mike recognized him, in spite of the fact that his curly ginger hair was plastered down straight and dark over his wet head: Ginger.

And now Ginger saw them and recognized them. 'Hi!' he shouted across the river, in his friendly way, and prepared to swing across to them on the rope.

He carried the operation out to perfection.

Four knots had been made in the rope at intervals, to suit the users of it. Ginger grasped the rope just above the third knot from the bottom, drew back from the edge of the river-bank in order to take a running leap, then ran – pushed off with both feet – and leapt forward over the water. His feet pushed and leapt and then clamped themselves about the rope just above the lowest knot, tied at the very end of it.

He came floating through the air on the rope, across the river, with the ease and grace of talent and practice. He landed faultlessly on the near bank, just beside Mike and Shirley. He steadied himself for an instant and then stood there, holding the rope.

He smiled directly at Mike; he really was a friendly boy. He said, 'Like a go?'

Mike was still able to think, to speak. He said, 'The others had better have their turns first . . .'

'Everyone's had a turn. It's all yours.'

Mike was rooted to the ground; his voice had vanished. But Shirley had moved forward hopefully; and Ginger, noticing her, said, 'You first, then?'

He showed her exactly where to hold on to the rope, above the particular knot that suited her height, and reminded her of the position of her feet above the lowest knot. He made her draw back from the edge of the bank, so that she could get a good run and push before swinging out and over. And he pointed out earnestly that she would need as much push from the other side to get back again. 'It's very important,' he said. 'If you miss your proper push from the bank – well, you've had it.'

'Yes,' said Shirley, again and again. 'Yes – yes – I know!' And she really did seem to understand, without more explanation. She held on to the rope just as she should and made her little run and push and leap and – gripping the rope with her feet – swung right across the river to land among Ginger's friends, who raised a mild cheer in her honour. Then she turned to swing back, but had not forgotten any of Ginger's instructions: holding the rope, she drew back, ran and pushed off across the river to land where Ginger and Mike stood on the other bank.

'That's it!' said Ginger; but, before he could say more, she was off again towards the far bank.

7

And then, expertly, back again. This time Ginger caught her and held her, while he took the rope from her. Mike watched, and knew what would happen next.

'Your turn,' Ginger said to him; and he had the same truly friendly smile as before.

Mike knew that everyone was looking at him: they were interested, but casual, knowing what they were expecting from him, not doubting they would have it from him. Only Shirley was perhaps looking at him in a different way, because she was his sister and she knew him: she knew what he might be thinking, feeling; she knew what he might do, what he might not do.

He tried to say aloud, 'No, I don't want to do it. I won't do it.' But he could not.

And Shirley watched his fear, his fear within fear.

Ginger was still holding the rope out towards him. Mike took it and stretched his hands up above the knot that Ginger said was for him. Blindly, he was about to set off on his swing at once; but Ginger pulled him back to make the necessary run up, leap and push.

So now he was away, swinging out from the near bank towards the far one; and one of his feet had come loose from its correct position above the bottom knot. The foot fumbled for its place again, and the rope tried to twist away from it, teasing it. And meanwhile he had left the near bank a long, long way behind and was over the middle of the river, and here came the far bank, taking him by cruel surprise. He still hadn't got both feet into the correct position, and that almost stupefied him with anxiety. He forgot the need to land properly on the far bank before starting his return swing. He remembered only the need to push off from it. His free foot touched the bank, and, at once, with all the strength of his one foot, he pushed and swung away again, rather unevenly, back towards the near bank. There was a wasteful twirl to his swing, and when he reached the other bank, where Ginger and Shirley stood, his toes only just touched it. With his toes he managed a push backwards, but too weakly to carry him the whole way back: at the end of his swing, his feet never touched the far bank at all. From that far bank, the automatic swing of a pendulum movement took him back towards the near bank, but with no possibility of his even touching it with his toes, far less of making a landing.

Now he swung towards the far bank; then back towards the near. To and fro he swung across the river, with no hope of making a landing on either bank.

Each time the swing became a little narrower. Narrower and narrower.

The rope, satisfied, now swung lazily and narrowly over the middle part of the river. Soon it would be hanging still, vertical, with Mike on it.

The swinging had narrowed to nothing. Stopped.

Mike was hanging on the rope over the middle of the river; and there was only one way in which he could stop hanging there and go home from this rope and river and meadow and hateful village. He must let go. His hands – and his remaining foot – must let go of the rope. He must fall into the river, which, after all, was not deep or swift-flowing; and he could swim.

He would not mind being in the river – oh, no! – but his hands would not let go of the rope. He whimpered to them to let go, but they would not. They gripped and clung and clutched in spite of the pain in the palms and an intolerable stretching of the muscles of his arms and a feeling as if his shoulders would split open.

He hung there on the rope, twirling slowly round over the middle of the river. Now he could see the people on the far bank: there were quite a lot of them, Ginger's friends and acquaintances, and they were all looking at him and giggling among themselves. Oh, yes! They were laughing all right! Now he couldn't see them any more, because he had rotated further, so that now he was facing the near bank, from which Ginger and Shirley were watching him. They watched in silence. And beyond them, coming across the meadow towards the rope, he saw two more people: his mother and his grandmother. They had finished the washing up and were coming to see how Mike and Shirley were enjoying themselves.

Suddenly, hanging there helplessly, he saw; he knew. He knew that nothing and nobody could save him now – unless he could save himself. He must do it immediately. At once. Now – now, before his mother and his grandmother reached the river-bank. His grandmother particularly.

One foot was already dangling: he detached the other from the rope, so that both feet hung free, although that made the agony in his hands and arms and shoulders even worse. He concentrated his will on letting go with his hands – of his own free will, before he was made to let go by pain and exhaustion. His will was prising open the fingers of his hands, and achieved it; and, in the split second of his falling, he also achieved the shout he willed himself to make. It came out partly as a scream, but it was also quite distinctly a word: 'Whoops!'

He was in the river. He was choking and drowning, but he surfaced; and it didn't matter that he was crying because he was all over water, anyway, or that he was sobbing, too, because he had to gasp for breath. Then he was swimming clumsily towards the near bank, and then wading, and finally clambering out to where his mother and grandmother and Shirley and Ginger waited for him.

His mother began fussing at once about his wetness and coldness and muddiness. But his grandmother boomed through it all: 'Well done, Mike! It doesn't matter a scrap that you didn't manage it first time! You were keen to have a go – that's the spirit! That's what I was like at your age! Well done!'

Ginger said nothing.

Shirley said nothing. She was looking at Mike, and

11

Mike knew that, because she was his sister, she knew things about him that nobody else did.

He just wanted to go home – to his own home. But that was impossible: he had to go back with the others to Gran's home, with his mother promising a hot bath and dry clothes, and his grandmother promising a tea with a very special summer treat. Apparently, while he and Shirley had been in the village buying comics, their grandmother and mother had been to a pick-your-own strawberry farm. There were strawberries and cream for tea. (The thought of it made Mike feel sick.)

Surprisingly, Ginger was coming, too. Mike supposed that his grandmother had bullied Ginger into that; or perhaps Ginger really wanted to come. Anyway, arrangements had been made about dry clothes and shoes or sandals or flip-flops for Ginger as well as for himself.

So they went home together. Shirley danced ahead in the triumph of her performance on the rope; then Gran, holding Ginger by her side in conversation; then Mum trailing a little behind, to encourage Mike; lastly, Mike – miserable Mike.

Later, Mike and Ginger were in the bath together. This had not been their idea, but by now Gran spoke of them together as 'the boys'. Because of her, they lay one at either end of her large bath, relaxing into the kindliness of hot, clean water. (They needed only to rinse off the river water, they had been told.) Now and then they shifted their limbs a little to start the ripples; they did not speak to each other.

Then, slyly, Ginger splashed at Mike, and Mike splashed back; and then they fooled around with the bathwater, until Mike sat up and looked over the side of the bath and wondered whether his grandmother would be pleased at the mess. Ginger also sat up to look, and said that his mother would have been furious.

Now they sat up at either end of the bath, facing each other, and Ginger said, 'Your mum said you were going home tomorrow.'

'Yes.'

'Will you come again?'

'Maybe.'

'I thought it was really good, that "Whoops!" when you fell in. I fell in once, when I was caught in the middle, early on. I wish I'd thought of "Whoops!" then.'

Mike said, 'If we come again, I shan't go on the rope again . . . I don't want to . . . I didn't want to, this afternoon . . .' He repeated fiercely, 'I tell you, I didn't want to!'

'You could have said,' said Ginger.

'No. I couldn't. I just couldn't.'

Ginger accepted this in silence, but thoughtfully.

The bathwater was cooling. Ginger, who sat at the tap-end, refreshed it with more hot water. Then he said, 'I'll tell you something about my dad.'

'Yes?'

'He's got a chain-saw. He cuts up wood. And once he nearly cut his thumb off. He had to go to hospital.'

'Oh, yes?'

'He nearly cut his thumb off.' Ginger began giggling uncontrollably. He was rocking with laughter, backwards and forwards in the bathwater, making waves that hit against Mike with a splash. He was almost screaming with laughter, and tears were running down his cheeks. He gasped out: 'There was an awful lot of blood everywhere, and when I saw it, I – I *fainted*.' On the last word, he became quite still and quiet, staring at Mike. He said, 'I haven't told anyone. You don't live here, and you're going away tomorrow.'

'We'll be coming back some day,' said Mike, 'because of our gran.'

'You won't tell,' said Ginger.

'No,' said Mike. He pondered. 'Blood – that's funny. Shirley fell out of a tree once and cut her head. She howled a lot, but she didn't mind the blood; nor did I.'

'Much blood?'

'Quite a bit. But I didn't mind.'

Ginger patted the surface of the bathwater with his hand. 'Funny . . .' he said.

Mike fished around in his mind for something his mother often remarked – nothing very witty or original, but just true: 'People are different,' he said.

Shirley came hammering on the door to tell them

the tea was made and the strawberries were on the table and she wanted to begin.

So they got out of the bath and dried and dressed as best they could and went downstairs together, to the kitchen. Tea was laid in the kitchen, on a table with a white cloth, and in the middle of the cloth was a huge bowl piled high with strawberries, ripe and red and shiny; there was cream in a jug; and sugar in a basin; and the sight did not make Mike feel sick.

Gran was sitting behind the teapot, and she was calling to them: 'Come in – come in, to a feast for heroes!'

So they went in to tea.

# Early Transparent

A grey squirrel impudently ran on the Chapmans' lawn – skipped and ran and then suddenly froze in attention. Then, as suddenly, it streaked towards a fruit tree and up into its invisibility.

The old man glared out on the scene from his invalid chair in the glassed-in veranda. His mouth had made a sound which was not intelligible to his wife or to his grandson standing by. But they recognized it as some word, and a word of rage.

'Why's Grandpa so angry?' whispered the boy.

His grandmother whispered back: 'They're thieves. They steal the fruit. Soon they'll be digging holes in the lawn for their nuts – *our* hazelnuts – against the

16

winter. Then, after all that, they forget where they've hidden them! Your grandfather has never had any patience with them.'

'Oh . . .'

'And that old war-wound troubles him more than ever. That puts his nerves on edge.'

She bent over the old man and kissed the top of his head so lightly that probably he did not know it.

So Nicky thought. He was on only a short visit to his grandparents. The last time he had stayed, his grandfather had been well and strong in spite of his age, and in spite of the war-wound that people were always going on about. He had not needed a wheel-chair; he had been clear in his speech – often bitingly clear when he complained or objected. In excuse for his short temper, the old lady would murmur yet again about his having been so badly wounded in the war – and, if he happened to overhear, he would blow up in scorching fury.

Now he was different, and Nicky was uneasy with the change.

But, anyway, Nicky would be home again soon. For his birthday. That looming event determined the longest he could possibly be expected to stay. His mother had said, 'Granny so loved having you visit – you remember the expeditions she used to take you on? And now she hardly gets out at all, because of Grandpa's being – well, because of Grandpa's being as he is. You could cheer her up; perhaps help her a bit.

17

Go to the shop for her, for instance. Garden. Odd jobs here and there. You're old enough.'

Nicky didn't like the idea of that; but he supposed that he could help a bit. Now they were moving back into the house from the veranda, leaving old Mr Chapman in his chair, still sitting in the sun. The veranda took most of the light from the living-room against which it had been built. The room was already shadowy and a little musty-smelling – but with a thin, fresh sweetness through the mustiness. A bowl of fruit stood in the middle of the big table.

Nicky said, 'Shall I go to the shop for you, Granny?'

She smiled at him delightedly: 'What a kind thought!' (Nicky shuffled his feet, knowing that the thought was only second-hand.) 'But everything's shut by now. And, anyway, you've come to enjoy yourself while you're here. Perhaps with Jeremy Gillespie? You get on so well, don't you? He's on holiday too, of course, and at home.'

'Oh, Jeremy . . . Yes . . .' Jeremy was the boy of about Nicky's age and only two houses along that his grandmother had decided would make the ideal holiday friend.

'But you'll have to wait until tomorrow for Jeremy. Then, after breakfast, there's a job for you both, to pick Early Transparents before the squirrels get them all. There's a bumper crop this year.' She took the bowl of fruit from the table – and the sweetness moved in the air as the fruit moved. She held the bowl under

Nicky's nose. 'Smell them. Then, before you eat one, try it against the light.'

Then came the little speech on the so-called transparency of these greengages – a speech always before made fretfully by his grandfather. But now his grandmother spoke it gently, almost laughing: 'Of course, they're not really *transparent*: you can't see right through them, as if they were made of glass. They're only *translucent*: you can see the light through the ripe ones. You should be able to see the darkness – the shadow – of the stone in the middle, against the light.'

Nicky held up one of the greengages against the sunset light from the veranda. He peered: 'I can't see any shadow.'

'You need to hold it against a better light. Tomorrow morning, perhaps.'

Neither of them mentioned the possibility of switching on the electric light. Artificial light was not what you used in testing an Early Transparent.

Nicky turned and turned the fruit, then gave up and popped it whole into his mouth. The resistance of the skin to his teeth, and then the almost-liquid rush of softness and sweetness! – For those few seconds he was dazed by Early Transparency.

He had even closed his eyes, and when he opened them again, his grandmother – to his astonishment – was in tears. She recovered herself instantly: 'I was just thinking of a child – of your mother as a child – of her picking Early Transparents.'

Nicky couldn't see the point of crying over a thing like that, but his grandmother was briskly going on: 'Now, if you and Jeremy find squirrels at the tree before you, don't try any tricks with them. They can be very vicious with those teeth!'

'Of course not, Granny,' said Nicky. His mind, however, was not on the squirrels but on Jeremy. The thought of sharing the picking of the first Early Transparents with Jeremy Gillespie depressed him. As his mother always pointed out, there was absolutely nothing wrong with Jeremy. Yet the idea of him lowered Nicky's spirits.

Cheerily now old Mrs Chapman promised him: 'You two can start picking straight after breakfast tomorrow morning. If it's fine.'

But it wasn't fine. Rain began in the night and continued most of the next day. Even before Nicky was down for breakfast, a new plan had had to be made on the telephone with Jeremy Gillespie's mother: the Early Transparents were postponed until tomorrow, and meanwhile Nicky and his grandmother would go shopping in the town centre. And no, Jeremy would not come with them because he wanted to work on his Holiday Project ('Oh,' said Nicky as neutrally as he could); and yes, all this meant old Mr Chapman would have been left alone in the house, but Mrs Chapman could get a friend to sit with him and give him his lunch.

In town they shopped, and Mrs Chapman bought

Nicky his birthday present – something he wanted and something of which she could approve. There was a craze for poster-making at the moment, so Nicky chose a set of coloured crayons, the rather expensive sort with brilliant, deep colours. Back home again, his grandmother first of all checked that his grandfather was all right and thanked the friend and said goodbye to her; then, enjoying herself, she set to wrapping the crayon-pack in birthday paper. 'You mustn't open the parcel until your birthday morning,' she told Nicky; and she put it inside his holiday suitcase to take home with him.

For the rest of that wet afternoon Nicky and his grandmother played board games and Nicky watched TV with his grandfather. (His grandmother said that she disliked what they showed on television now-adays.) In any fine interval they could glimpse the squirrels towards the bottom of the garden, where the greengage tree grew just out of sight. 'They'll be at the Early Transparents,' his grandmother sighed. 'Well, at least, this year, there's plenty for all.'

That night, at sunset, the sky was red, which gave old Mrs Chapman much satisfaction: 'Shepherd's de-light,' she said, meaning a fine day to come. And her husband, who had apparently heard and understood her, gave a loud exclamation unmistakably of scorn, so that she whispered to Nicky, 'He means I talk *poppy-cock* – that's always been his word. I irritate him,' she added humbly.

But the evening's weather forecast bore out Mrs Chapman's hopes; and she telephoned the Gillespies to remake arrangements for the next day.

As he listened to her on the telephone, Nicky found a wild resolve forming in his mind. His grandmother had always stressed that they could start picking only after breakfast. But, saying nothing to anybody, Nicky would begin picking *before* breakfast – well before breakfast, and before Jeremy Gillespie could possibly be turning up. That meant getting up really early; but after all, these were *Early* Transparents, weren't they? So the early morning seemed right.

Moreover, quite alone, he would be able to eat morning fruit fresh from the tree.

After supper, Granny had to get Grandpa to bed, and she was already tired by the morning's shopping. So they were all in bed in very good time – Nicky much earlier than he would have been at home. He did not mind that, because he supposed he would wake earlier; and so he did.

He lay in bed, listening carefully. From his grand-parents' bedroom, two snores: one a regular, gentle sighing sound; the other rasping and deep with an occasional snuffling exclamation – old Mr Chapman suffered from dreams of the war in which he had fought years ago. Sometimes he used actually to scream aloud and wake himself – and his wife – from a night-mare. But not tonight.

And the night was really over by now. Cautiously

Nicky got out of bed and dressed to let himself out into the garden.

There he found himself in a hushed time between birdsong and the start of human activity. He did not wish to disturb this quiet. He trod measuredly over the wet grass. He saw no raiding squirrels as he went. He reached the end of the garden, where the Early Transparent tree grew in a corner where garden fencing met hedge.

The branches of the tree were bowed down with the fruit as he had never seen them before. Last year there had been only a very poor crop; the year before that he had not even been here at the right time; and before that – well, he could not certainly remember. But this year! His grandmother had said 'plenty' – and oh! the plenitude of it, the brimming abundance, the *munificence*! The morning sunshine lit up the fruit everywhere – larger than ordinary greengages and plump, with the lightest of blooms breathed on the skins and a freckling of red. Ripe, ready, and so many – so many!

As he gazed, one particular fruit seemed to present itself to him, to invite him. He stretched out his hand and touched it and, at his touch, it fell into the palm of his hand. He held it up between finger and thumb towards the sun, and the morning sunlight shone through it, and – yes, this time he saw clearly the shadow of the stone at the very heart of the fruit.

And, out of the corner of his eye, saw something

else. Hardly a movement – a *presence*. And looked past the fruit he was holding and met the fixed gaze of eyes. Not the eyes of any wild creature, but wild all the same, with a stare of terror. He saw – how could he have missed it earlier? – a child who stood absolutely still among the leaves and branches and looked at him and also through him and beyond him with that stare of horror. The child was clutching a handful of Early Transparents to its chest.

Their gaze was locked, without wink or blink, until Nicky drew breath. Then: 'You're stealing!' he accused. 'Stealing!' he repeated in a shout, because he was somehow frightened by the child. The child's mouth opened as if it might speak, but did not; and the mouth remained open, a little black hole of silence. And the eyes still stared and stared.

As though his shout had raised an alarm, a door banged distantly from the direction of the house and his grandmother's voice was calling his name – calling to him again and again and (he realized) coming swiftly closer. He turned his head towards the sound and when he turned his gaze back, the child had gone. Where it had been, the leaves were still moving; but the child had gone.

'What are you doing? Oh, what are you doing?' his grandmother was calling, and now he saw her. She was still in her nightdress, and running barefoot over the wet grass towards him, her grey hair uncombed, unarranged.

24

She reached him; she clutched him. 'Nicky, what have you *done*?'

'There was someone stealing your Early Transparents.'

'The child — only the child. Only a little girl.' His grandmother began to weep, just as she had wept so unexpectedly on the day of his arrival. 'She thinks nobody knows that she comes. But I know, and I don't mind — no, I'm glad for her, poor child.'

'But, Granny —'

His grandmother was rushing on. 'She's come to stay with some cousin who lives down the road. There's no one else where she comes from; her family all dead, all killed. Nicky, she was found underneath them all, the only one left alive; and since then she doesn't speak. She can't speak. And she stares . . .'

His grandmother's headlong, sobbing speech bewildered Nicky. But now they both heard from the house the irregular ringing of a bell — the bell that always stood within close reach of Mr Chapman, in case he needed anything or anyone. The ringing sounded impatient, angry.

'I must go to him,' said Mrs Chapman, calming herself. Without another word, she turned and ran back to the house. Nicky followed her. He had no more thought of the Early Transparents. He found the one he had picked to eat still in his hand when he reached the house. Violently he flung it towards the bottom of the garden for the squirrels to find.

Old Mr Chapman's getting up and dressed and to the breakfast table was a slow and difficult business. He was cantankerous, and kept his wife busy until the very end of breakfast. By then Jeremy Gillespie had arrived, which seemed to annoy the old man further. (Fortunately Jeremy Gillespie did not notice.)

The picking was to begin at once. Mrs Chapman gave each boy a basket, and Jeremy set off immediately towards the bottom of the garden. She held Nicky back for a moment, while she put a finger to her lips. He nodded.

All the same, while they were picking, he said casually, 'My granny says there's a funny girl staying down this road – I mean, she's strange. So my gran says.'

'She's foreign,' said Jeremy. 'Quite young. Staying with some distant relative. Nobody sees her. She doesn't go out. She's too scared.'

'What's she scared of?'

'She's a refugee,' said Jeremy, as though that explained everything.

'But where's she a refugee from? Why's she one?' asked Nicky.

Jeremy was growing impatient of this conversation. 'Some war zone abroad – civil war. It was all on telly ages ago.'

Nicky didn't quite disbelieve his grandmother, but she could get things muddled. He asked, 'But what *happened*?'

'Soldiers. They burnt the village. They shot everybody. They killed all this girl's family. There was a pile of dead bodies, but the girl was underneath everybody, so she wasn't killed. People rescued her, and she was brought to this country because of the relative here. Don't you ever follow the news?'

'Not really,' said Nicky.

'We do Current Affairs at my school,' said Jeremy Gillespie.

When they had filled their baskets, they went back to the house. Mrs Chapman weighed her share of the fruit and prepared to make greengage jam. Jeremy Gillespie took his share home, but Nicky said he would stay with his grandmother and help her with the jam. Jeremy Gillespie did not seem to mind: he said that at home he could begin to finalize his Project.

Nicky would have enjoyed the jam-making, but he and his grandmother worked almost in silence. She refused absolutely to talk about what had happened that morning at the greengage tree. When he tried her with even one question, she wept again. He had only been wondering whether the little girl might ever come again. He would like to have said he was sorry. He would like to have said something that perhaps would make things better for her. He would like to have *done* something.

He could have given her something, as a present. Perhaps even his own birthday crayons. But he knew that a present was a stupid idea – stupid! A present wouldn't make up for not having a mother or a father or anyone else any more. All your family killed and lying dead on top of you; you underneath them all, alive. Oh, a present was a stupid idea – stupid – stupid!

He tried not to think of the little girl. He thought of the greengage jam he was helping to make. There would be a pot of it to take home to his family. And when he got home there would be planning for his birthday the next day. And the next day would *be* his birthday . . .

He was going home tomorrow. This was his last night in his grandmother's house. Later, in bed, he thought of being at home again, and of his birthday and his birthday party and all the presents. And suddenly he was thinking again of the little girl at the Early Transparent tree and of her stare that looked at him and through him and far beyond him. It was true that nothing could ever make up for what had happened to her in that country where she had once lived. Nothing.

In the quietness of the night he lay listening to the snoring of his grandparents in their bedroom.

After a while he slipped out of bed and rummaged in his case until he found the birthday crayons. He decided to unwrap them, so that it would be quite plain what they were and that at least they were harmless. The rustling of his unwrapping sounded so loud that he was afraid it might waken the sleepers, but they snored on.

Carrying the crayons, he crept downstairs and out of

the house. This was truly night-time; but by starlight he could still see his way down to the Early Transparent tree. He reached the tree and set the crayons on the grass at its foot, then thought that they might look accidental – left there by mistake. So he picked fruit from the tree and heaped it on top; then thought the squirrels would take the fruit, anyway. So he reversed the heap, with the crayon pack balanced on top of the fruit.

Then he went back to the house and to bed. There was still the same snoring from his grandparents' bedroom, one snore gently sighing, the other seeming to snatch at each rasping breath as though it were its last. As he listened, it seemed to him that probably, after all, he had just done a stupid, stupid thing. He fell asleep, half-wishing that he had not done what he had done.

The next morning, after breakfast, the usual friend came to be with old Mr Chapman, so that Mrs Chapman could see Nicky off on the train.

Nicky positioned himself in front of his grandfather and said his goodbye. The old man looked at him and it seemed to Nicky that his grandfather also looked through him and beyond him. But at least he spared his grandson a wintry smile. That done, and at the last moment: 'I'd like to take an Early Transparent for the journey,' said Nicky.

'Take several from the bowl,' said his grandmother. 'Hurry!' But Nicky was already on his way down to the tree itself. When he had almost reached it, he stopped. He daren't look. He so wanted this to be all right after all. Just this one little thing.

He looked. And there was nothing at the foot of the Early Transparent tree. She had come, after all, and she had taken his gift.

He picked his Early Transparents for the journey and rushed back to the house.

Later, in the train, he thought of the crayons and their intense colours and what you could do with them, and he thought that perhaps – just perhaps – she really would use them, and enjoy them, as he would have done. He hoped so.

# The Fir Cone

The door of what was now Charlie's cupboard would not shut.

Not a crisis, you might think. Not even a tricky situation, really.

Certainly absurd for a mother to think of a *trap* of any kind. So Mrs Waring reassured herself, controlling her breathing. She had to deal only with a cupboard over-full of old toys.

She dragged forward her huge, empty cardboard box (the carton in which a new school TV had been delivered). She had supposed that she and her carton and – of course – Charlie himself would be alone together in front of the cupboard. But here were her two elder children as well: Sandra and Bill had drifted downstairs quite separately, it appeared, but as though both expected something interesting. Sandra leant against one door-jamb, attending minutely to a fingernail; Bill leant on the other side, staring and chewing in the way that particularly irritated Mrs Waring.

She decided to ignore the onlookers.

'Now, Charlie,' she said. 'Let's just see.'

She laid her hand flat on the cupboard door and pressed steadily. The door went back; it even seemed to click shut for a moment. Then, the hand-pressure released, it sprang open again, gaping wider than before. Something small fell lightly from the cupboard to the floor and rolled a little.

'There!' said Mrs Waring. 'You see what I mean? An old fir cone that one of you was hoarding. Absolute rubbish. The door won't shut because of all the stuff in the cupboard, and most of it rubbish!'

She had stepped forward to pick up the fir cone, but Charlie was before her – picked it up and put it into his pocket. 'Mine,' he said. His hand remained in his pocket, round the fir cone, feeling its broken tips, its age. Long ago he had picked it up under the great green tent of its parent tree. There were ducks quacking at a little distance – they had a whole lake to swim about on. And he had picked up his fir cone and kept it ever since.

Charlie was now standing between his mother and the cupboard, and the cupboard door was slowly swinging open to its widest.

The inside of the cupboard became visible to them all. It was crammed. Along the front edge of the top shelf lay an exhausted doll, one arm dangling down towards the next shelf; lower, a fire-engine, unmanned; a skipping-rope frayed almost to a thread in the middle; some sea-shells in a see-through raffia bag; a climbing monkey with the remains of his ladder; a dirty Hallowe'en outfit crammed into a shoebox; several My Pretty Ponies —

'Such old, old stuff!' Mrs Waring was saying. 'Outgrown, all of it! Now, Charlie, I promised I wouldn't throw out anything that belonged to you, without your permission. But wouldn't you like some of your better things — say, the fire-engine that you never play with now — to go into the jumble sale?' (The school jumble sale was being held that afternoon.) 'Wouldn't you like some other, younger child to enjoy one of your old toys? Wouldn't you, Charlie?'

'No,' said Charlie, 'I wouldn't. I just hate other younger children.'

Mrs Waring sighed. She braced herself again and took a firmer grip of her carton. 'All right, then. We'll just get rid of the rubbishy stuff that belonged to Sandra and Bill years ago.'

'No,' said Charlie.

'But Sandra and Bill don't want any of it now,' said Mrs Waring. She turned sharply on them: 'You don't, do you?'

'Oh, no,' said Sandra, and Bill said, 'No concern of

ours at all now.' There was something about the way Bill said that last word – something in the way they both *watched* that made Mrs Waring feel uneasy.

She turned back to Charlie. 'So we'll just get rid of their stuff, anyway.' She had the doll in mind. She stepped towards the cupboard.

Charlie sprang in front of it, his arms spread wide in its defence: 'No!'

Mrs Waring remained reasonable. 'Remember, Charlie, I've promised I won't get rid of anything that belongs to you.' (Mrs Waring prided herself on her *straightness* with her children: she always said that a promise was a promise.) 'Only Sandra's old stuff and Bill's will go –'

'No,' said Charlie. 'You can't take anything. You haven't my permission. And it *all* belongs to me – all of it.'

'That's not true,' said Mrs Waring.

'Yes, it is,' said Charlie. 'Because they've given me all of their stuff. So it does all belong to me.' He added, 'Since last night.' He glanced at Sandra and Bill.

Bill said, 'Yeah. It was last night.'

Mrs Waring tried to speak, but could not.

Sandra looked almost sorry for her mother. She said, 'Charlie just asked us to give him all the old toy-cupboard stuff that was ours, and we did. So you see . . .'

There was what seemed a long silence, a stillness, in which they were all looking at their mother.

34

Then Mrs Waring groaned; she knew that she had been beaten. Charlie was saying, over and over again, loudly, 'You've promised – you've promised – you've promised –'

Sandra said, 'You needn't be so mean about it, Charlie.' And to her mother: 'I think I might make us some tea.'

Bill said, 'I'll look after the box.' He began to drag it from the room.

Their mother said faintly, 'It might as well go out with the dustbins.'

The three of them left Charlie kneeling in front of his toy-cupboard, alone in his triumph.

For a while he gloated.

He had wanted everything – or rather, he had wanted everything to stay there. To stay there for always.

He remembered the fir cone in his pocket, and thought of putting it back in the cupboard, but the fir cone – the feel of it under his fingers in his pocket – made him think back to the ducks and the lake and the tent-tree. Across the grass to the great tree his mother and father had danced him between them. They were all three breathless from laughing. And he had picked up his fir cone and kept it ever since.

This very afternoon his father would be saying to him, 'What shall we do? Where shall we go?' and he could answer that he wanted to go back – back to the tree and the lake and the ducks and the happiness.

His father had been there, so he would know the place.

This afternoon his mother would be at the school jumble sale, organizing.

He could hear his mother in the kitchen, talking to Sandra – but Sandra was doing most of the talking, in a soothing sort of voice.

He began to wish that he hadn't, perhaps, been so hard – yes, perhaps, so *mean* – to his mother; but, on the other hand, it had, perhaps, been necessary. And, anyway, perhaps, it wasn't too late. Thoughtfully he took the shoebox out of the cupboard and removed the Hallowe'en kit. Then he began to put into the box a few of the things he could, after all, most easily spare, perhaps: certainly the doll, and a couple of the Ponies, several of the less attractive sea-shells from their bag . . . .

The voices from the kitchen continued. They had been joined by Bill.

Bill was laughing, chuckling away.

Charlie heard his name and began to listen intently, his hands still over the partly-filled shoebox.

Bill was saying, 'What a kid! You have to hand it to him!'

Sandra said, 'It was childish – childish!'

His mother, steady-voiced by now, said, 'Partly I blame myself. For he is still a child, after all – very young for his age, too . . .'

Charlie scooped everything out of the shoebox and thrust it back into the cupboard. His hands were trembling with anger. He left the box and the Hallowe'en stuff on the floor and the cupboard door wide open, and stamped his way out of the room and up the stairs.

They heard him – they could not have failed to. The voices from the kitchen stopped. Then his mother called, 'Charlie, remember: you're not to go to meet your father without Sandra.' And Sandra said something about being ready soon. She spoke in that soothing voice that Charlie hated.

He went on hating his sister, with fervour but in sullen silence.

Later that morning, sitting in the Tube going across London, with Sandra beside him as escort, Charlie still hated his sister; but he was thinking ahead to the meeting with his father. Would he be there? Once he hadn't been – missed the coach, he said. Then Charlie would have been stranded, if Sandra or Bill hadn't been with him. That's what his mother had said afterwards to his father on the telephone. And his father had said back –

Oh, Charlie thought, he was sick of them both. And of Sandra and Bill.

All the same, he did want to be with his father again. And he thrust his hand into his pocket and felt the fir cone there and remembered the ducks and the lake and the happiness.

And, anyway, at the coach station his father was there, just descended from the coach and looking about him – and saw Charlie – and then Sandra with him: 'Sandy!'

But Sandra said hurriedly, 'Sorry, Dad –' and then about some friends she was due to go out with. Charlie could tell that his father was really disappointed, and he asked after Bill (who was at his Saturday afternoon match). Then Sandra said goodbye and left Charlie and his father to their afternoon together.

It was beginning to rain, and his father said they might as well start with something to eat, and Charlie chose Chinese. When the noodles and the bamboo shoots and all the rest were eaten, Charlie sat back in his chair and smiled at his father, and his father smiled back at him. The moment seemed just right, so Charlie said that what he'd *really* like to do next was go somewhere they'd been before – a special place; and (feeling for the fir cone in his pocket) he mentioned the tree and the lake and the ducks.

'I don't know what it was called, but we went there by train. You and me and – and Mum.' Casually he brought the fir cone from his pocket and trundled it among the bottles of soy sauce and other things.

'By train?' said his father. 'So it was outside London?'

'I don't know, really,' said Charlie. 'And when we got there we had to pay to get in. But there wasn't a queue to get in, although you kept saying there would be. Oh, and there were animals – strange beasts. In a row.'

'It sounds like Whipsnade Zoo, if there were wild animals and it was outside London. But I don't remember us ever taking you to Whipsnade . . .' His father frowned, pondering.

Charlie said, 'And there was a gapoda.'

'*A what?*'

Charlie repeated, but in a fluster, 'A gappy-something.' In his fright he gestured aimlessly with his hand and knocked over the soy sauce bottle and that sent flying a little bunch of wooden toothpicks. 'A gadopa. As tall, as high as a house, and with sticky-out bits all the way up, like – like fins.'

Suddenly his father was angry. 'What rubbish you talk! A boy of your age! I only hope it isn't something your mother –'

He broke off with the same suddenness. 'Look, Charlie, we've only got the afternoon, and it's raining hard. We can't go far, and it might be better not to get too wet. Right?'

Shakily Charlie said, 'All right.'

'So what about a cinema?'

'All right.'

'And I'll get us some popcorn.'

'All right – I mean, thank you,' said Charlie.

So they went to the cinema and ate popcorn and watched a horror film that Charlie chose; and afterwards they had quite a large snack in a snack-bar. By then Charlie was rather enjoying his afternoon, after all; but by now his father was saying it was time to

39

deliver Charlie back home, and get himself back to the coach station.

They went home by way of the school, because Charlie said his mother might still be at the jumble sale.

'All right,' said his father.

And so she was.

They went in through the school gate as the last of the jumble sale shoppers were coming out. One or two said 'Hello!' to Charlie, but nobody greeted his father. It was so long ago that he used sometimes to be at the school gate.

As soon as they entered the assembly hall, Charlie remembered the smell of other jumble sales. There was a dustiness, and an *oldness* and a kind of under-smell that Mrs Waring always said angrily was the smell of unwashed clothes. (The clothes that her children had grown out of were always washed and even ironed before she allowed them to go as jumble.)

All the chairs usually in the hall had been packed away, replaced by big trestle tables on which the jumble – mostly clothes, some china and books and toys – had been laid out. People had queued to be first into the sale when the doors opened. Then they had stormed in and rushed at the tables and scrabbled and clawed to get whatever was worth getting before someone else reached it.

So by now – the end of the afternoon – very little was left, and a good deal of that was on the floor and trampled on. The only person still sorting through and still haggling to buy this or that for a very few pence was the old rag-woman.

The jumble sale helpers were still there, of course, fed up but at least satisfied because the sale was over and it was only a matter of counting the money taken. And centrally among the trestles stood Charlie's mother, who was the organizer. Her arms and hands dangled as though their muscles were exhausted with the battle against snatch-and-grab. Her hair was all over the place, and her face was tired.

She saw Charlie and she smiled, and then abruptly stopped smiling, and Charlie knew that she had caught sight of his father standing behind him.

'Well?' she called.

Charlie edged past the trestle tables to reach her.

'Well?' she repeated.

'We went to the pictures,' said Charlie, 'and we ate Chinese. I had sweet-sour and fried noodles and – and –' (he knew he would get it wrong, because now he was nervous) 'and – you know – shampoo boots –'

'*What?*' said his mother.

Charlie knew that he could not speak again. If he tried, then he might begin to cry.

'Bamboo shoots,' said his father from behind him. He said nothing else at all, but his hand touched the back of Charlie's neck and Charlie knew that meant, Goodbye until next time. And Charlie did not turn to see him go.

'Charlie,' said his mother, 'I can't come away at once, but I shan't be long. You can go the rest of the way home by yourself, can't you? It's only a step. Sandra will still be there and she'll let you in.'

'Yes,' said Charlie. 'All right.' But he did not move: he stood there, his hands in his pockets.

'Is something wrong?' asked his mother. 'What is it, Charlie?'

'Nothing,' said Charlie in a choked voice. 'Nothing.'

Nothing in either pocket, where his hand had searched for comfort.

Nothing; and in his mind's eye he saw the Chinese tablecloth and the muddle of empty dishes and the toppled soy sauce bottle and the scatter of toothpicks, and somewhere in that confusion he had left his fir cone.

Because of the fuss about the gapoda, because his father had shouted at him, he had lost his head and forgotten all about his fir cone. Forgotten it. Left it. *Lost it*.

'Charlie –' his mother began, but Charlie had already turned away – was gone. He ran headlong for home. It seemed to him that he reached it only in the nick of time, for the sobbing was beginning. He put his finger on the bell and kept it there, so that the bell rang and rang and rang through the house.

Sandra, in the bathroom, had just finished washing her hair for her evening out. The screaming of the bell

42

irritated her, for she was late – oh! she was always late – and it could only be Charlie down there. She wrapped her hair in a towel-turban and sailed downstairs to open the door. By now the ringing had ceased, but only because someone was hammering at the door – hammer – hammer – hammer with bare fists –

'*What on earth –*' she cried as she flung open the door; but then she staggered back, speechless, as Charlie flung himself inside in a storm of weeping. He landed up in his sister's arms, for she was too startled to remember her irritation; and he was too distraught to care about anything.

Clutching him in alarm, Sandra said, 'What is it, Charlie? What's happened? Was it Dad? Did he say something awful?'

'I've lost it!' Charlie sobbed. 'Now I shall never go there!'

'Lost what? Go where? Oh, Charlie, what's the matter?'

'They'll say we never went there. They'll say there's no such place. They'll say I made it all up. Dad thinks that. Mum will, too. But there was such a place. There was – there was!'

'What place, Charlie? Try not to cry, and then you can tell me properly. Tell me about it – just tell me, Charlie!'

Charlie calmed himself enough to tell her. About the lake and the ducks and the tent-tree and the gapoda-building and the stone monsters. 'And we went there by train and all the time Dad was singing a little song he'd just made up about queuing to get in and Mum was laughing – and we didn't have to queue, anyway. We just paid some money and walked in.'

Sandra had been listening very attentively. Now she asked, 'Were there greenhouses, Charlie? Big ones – enormous?'

'Yes, I forgot about those. We went into one, but it was too steamy-hot and full of huge plants right up to its roof. I liked it better outside.'

'Charlie, this is important. Think carefully about the song Dad made up about queuing: what *exactly* did he sing?'

Rather fretfully, Charlie said, 'I've just told you.'

'Try to remember the exact words. The *exact* words, Charlie.'

'Well . . . He sang over and over again: "We'll be queueing – queueing – queueing –" No, it wasn't quite that. He sang: "We'll have to queue – to queue – to queue –" Something like that.'

'You're sure it wasn't "We're going to . . ." instead of "We'll have to . . ."?'

'That's it,' agreed Charlie. 'It's easier to sing, isn't it? "We're going to queue – to queue – to queue –"' He broke off suddenly: 'But it doesn't *matter*, all that.' His tears began to fall again.

Sandra clutched him and shook him, to make him listen. 'It does matter, Charlie – it does! Because on the other side of London there's a place called Kew, with gardens – the most enormous gardens, with huge trees and huge glasshouses and a lake with ducks and a Chinese pagoda – not a gapoda, Charlie! – and you get to Kew Gardens by a special railway – the North London Railway. Oh, and the stone monsters are from the Queen's Coronation, ages ago. And that's where you went – that's what Dad was singing: "We're going to Kew – to Kew – to Kew –"'

Charlie stared at her, angrily. 'How do you know all that? You've just made it up. It's not true.'

'It is true. Because I went. There was a school expedition for the Infants. Just to Kew Gardens.'

'Why didn't Bill ever go with a school expedition to Kew?'

'He did, when he was an Infant.'

'Then why didn't I go when I was an Infant?'

'Because you were having chicken-pox. They didn't tell you what you were missing. But when you were all right again, I suppose Mum and Dad thought they'd take you anyway, all on your own.'

'So the place is really there . . .' He believed her now. 'So I could go with them again some day.'

'Well, no,' said Sandra.

'No?'

'Charlie, you know perfectly well they wouldn't take you, not the two of them together. Dad would take you, or Mum would. But not both of them together. Not now. Never again.'

'Never again . . .' said Charlie.

While they were speaking, the front gate had clanged and footsteps hurried to the front door, which Charlie had not closed behind him. Bill now flung it wide as he rushed in, dishevelled, excited by his afternoon, and roared up the stairs. He shouted back to them that he'd only come to collect something, then he was off again with his mates. They must tell Mum what he was up to.

'Up to!' Sandra murmured satirically, as she began to unwind her turban to shake out her damp hair. 'Charlie, I must go. I'm late already. Mum'll be back any minute now. Then you'll be all right.' She went back upstairs.

Charlie was left standing by the front door, while upstairs buzzed with blithe preparations for departure.

He was still grieving at loss: he had lost his fir cone . . . (Bill roared past him again on his way out: 'Eer chup, Misery! It may never happen!' Charlie easily worked out what that was supposed to mean. Only the stale old tease.)

But at least he had gained knowledge. There was a song – only a little song, but now it made sense: the Kew song. And it had power in it, too. A chant, an incantation, a spell . . . (Sandra swept down the stairs: 'You OK now?' She did not wait for an answer but was through the hall and out through the front door, calling back to him: 'Wait in for Mum, remember!' The front door clicked shut behind her.)

Abruptly the house was silent. Empty except for Charlie.

He stood there, thinking for a while. Then he shut his eyes, and opened his mouth to whisper: 'I'm going to Kew – to Kew – to Kew –'

He stood on soft green turf and the gardens lay before him: the glasshouses (he did not forget them this time) and the Queen's Beasts and the Chinese pagoda and the lake and the ducks and the great green tent-trees. And the people – all visitors to the gardens, and among them a little boy being jumped along between his parents. All three were laughing, and, when the child was set down, he stooped and picked up a fir cone and put it into his pocket . . .

'That's me,' said Charlie aloud, and was amazed to think how small – how very *young* – he had been. He might go to Kew again; but he could never be that age again, and do those things again that a little boy could do with his mum and his dad. With his mum and his dad who had been happy to be together with him. Sandra had said, Never again. And he saw now why she had said that.

He opened his eyes, and stood for a moment, thinking. His mother would be back any moment; he hadn't much time. He moved swiftly from the hall into the kitchen and then out by the back door to where the dustbins stood.

When Mrs Waring walked in, the hall was empty. She called anxiously up the stairs: 'Charlie?'

'Here!' The answer was from downstairs. She pushed open a door, and there he was, kneeling in front of his old toy-cupboard with the big TV carton beside him. He was packing it with objects from the cupboard.

'Oh, Charlie!' His mother sounded as if she might begin to cry.

He couldn't bear more of that. Without turning round, he said in a voice that he made cruel: 'Of course, you realize it's all far too late for your jumble sale? You realize that?'

'Oh, no, it isn't, Charlie – at least, it's too late for the school one, but there are lots of jumble sales going on all the time, every Saturday. I can always take good jumble somewhere useful.'

Still packing the carton, still not looking at his mother, he asked lightly: 'Mum, do you remember when I was very little I had chicken-pox?'

'Of course. Why?'

'Afterwards, you took me to Kew Gardens. You and Dad. We had a lovely time.'

The expression on her face had changed; she said coldly, 'Oh?'

'A *really* lovely time. Don't you remember?' He had turned round to search her face with his gaze.

'With your father?' Mrs Waring would have liked to deny any such memory; but – just as a promise is a promise – truth is truth. She sighed. 'Yes, just the three of us – I do remember; and we did have a lovely time. But that's in the past, Charlie, and –'

48

He interrupted her impatiently: 'I know all that stuff about you and Dad nowadays. You've explained before. But I just wanted to know that you remembered that time. Because at least it really happened. It did.'

'Of course it did,' said his mother, and had the feeling – which she did not always have – that she had said a good thing as well as a correct one.

'So that's all right,' said Charlie. He got up from his knees. 'I can finish the cupboard after tea.' With a deep sigh he stretched his arms to their utmost, as though he had been cramped for a long, long time.

Then, comfortingly: 'What's for tea, Mum?'

# Nutmeg

The little black dog called Peppercorn died of old age at last, and the children of the family – Lydia and Joe and little Sam – buried him. The first that their neighbours, the Copleys, knew of all this was the doleful sound of 'Abide with Me' coming in through Margaret Copley's bedroom window. She urged her husband to go out into the garden to see what the Tillotsons were up to.

The Tillotsons' garden had a neglected patch at the bottom, overrun with ivy, where snowdrops came up at the end of winter. Here the children had buried the body and were just setting up a home-made wooden cross, with 'Pepper' scratched on its horizontal.

('Peppercorn' was too long and, anyway, the little dog had always been called Pepper for short.)

George Copley peeped cautiously over the fence, but the children's father, also a spectator, spotted him at once. He waved his hand towards the little group of mourners. 'All the fun of a funeral!' he whispered.

Mr Copley was elderly. He and his wife had no children. He stared over the fence, wonderingly. 'You mean, they don't really care?'

'Oh, Lyddy does – just for now. The other two are too young, anyway.'

Lydia had heard him. She had been crying. Now she turned and shouted at her father: 'It's not just for now! And I hate you!'

'Temper!' said Mr Copley from over the fence, and then, alarmed at his own boldness, withdrew and went indoors to tell his invalid wife about the strange customs of the Tillotson family.

Meanwhile, Mrs Tillotson was calling everyone in for tea. The children ran in ahead of their father. As Lydia passed him, she said savagely: 'And you needn't think I'll ever want another dog after Pepper. Ever.'

Her father laughed, amused, tolerant.

Lydia had loved Pepper.

But later that same year old Mr Copley observed Lydia and the others playing in their garden with a new puppy. Mr Copley was no more used to dogs than to children, so only one question seemed safe over the fence. He asked, 'What are you going to call it?'

'Not *it*,' said Joe. 'Him. This is a boy dog, Mr Copley.'

'And we haven't decided what to call him,' said Lydia. She picked up the puppy, soft and plump, and cuddled him almost under her chin. At the sight, Mr Copley was reminded of many years ago, of the child – the only child – he and his wife had had. He remembered how his wife had held the baby against her breast, bending her head low and lovingly. Their child had died in infancy.

'Let me have him!' clamoured Sam, and Lydia lowered the puppy into the little boy's arms. There he wriggled and bit with needle-teeth until Sam squeaked with pain, but he would not give the puppy up. 'I want to call him Cuddles,' he said.

'Salt,' said Joe. 'To match Pepper.'

'No!' cried Lydia; and then: 'He's not the colour of salt, anyway.' The puppy was a rather unusual brown colour.

'Cuddles,' said Sam.

'We'll let you know, if you like, when we've decided,' Lydia told Mr Copley.

Later, indoors, their father explained to Sam: 'You have to choose a dog's name that you can *call*. You couldn't really call "Cuddles".' He raised his voice, deliberately comic: "Cuddles! Cuddles! Come here, Cuddles!"' Lydia and Joe laughed; Sam sulked, but he knew he was beaten.

It was their mother who had the brainwave. 'He's

just the colour of ground nutmeg. Why not call him Nutmeg? It's a kitchen name, like Peppercorn.'

The two boys liked the idea; Lydia hesitated.

'Meg for short,' said Joe, and Sam agreed.

'That's really a girl's name,' objected Lydia.

'Come on, Lyddy!' said her father. 'Why on earth should that matter, for a dog?'

So Lydia gave way, and the Tillotsons began training their new dog, Nutmeg – house-training him and training him to come when he was called. Their garden rang with the new name: Meg – Meg – Meg –

Margaret Copley, in her invalid's bedroom, managed a weak laugh as she listened to the children's voices distantly calling. George Copley did not even smile, because his wife's illness frightened him: he suspected that she was dying. His wife knew that she was.

Before the end of that summer, Margaret Copley had died.

Mr Copley's niece came to the funeral and afterwards tried to persuade the old man to come and live with her family. He would not budge.

'He simply won't budge,' Mrs Tillotson reported to her husband. She had been chatting with Mr Copley's niece. 'Well, he's lived all his married life in that house. Nearly fifty years.'

'It's a big change for him to get used to,' agreed Mr Tillotson. 'He'll just have to put the past behind him. Forget.'

Lydia noticed that her mother said nothing, but looked doubtful.

The Tillotson children, out in the garden all day with their new puppy, spared hardly a thought for their bereaved neighbour. These were the school holidays: there was all the time in the world for playing with Nutmeg – playing with him and training him. 'Meg! Meg! Meg!' they called, getting him used to his name.

One afternoon when they had been calling, scolding and coaxing, Mr Copley stuck his head over the fence to address them. He was white-faced and wild-haired. 'Would you mind, please – I'm sure you wouldn't – not calling your dog all the time? Just don't use that name over and over again. Please.'

All three of them stopped what they were doing – even Nutmeg stopped racing round; they stared at the old man. Then Lydia said, 'But we need to call him, Mr Copley. We're training him to come when he's called.'

'There's no need about it!' said Mr Copley, suddenly loud-voiced. He struck the top of the fence with his walking-stick. '*Stop that calling, I say! Stop it!*'

Then, astonishingly, the walking-stick came sailing over the fence towards them, unmistakably thrown with ill-will. It missed the little group, but the Tillotson children snatched up their puppy and scurried indoors to safety and to report what had happened.

Sam was crying, but Lydia and Joe were more startled than frightened.

Their mother was startled and also alarmed for Mr Copley himself. 'The poor man sounds half out of his mind,' she said, and resolutely made a Victoria sponge and took it round to his house. She rang the front-door bell, but Mr Copley saw her through a side-window and would not come to the door. As she had seen him seeing her, Mrs Tillotson left the sponge-cake on the front doorstep, hoping that he would recognize it as a peace-offering.

The children's father, when he heard the story, was furiously angry about the walking-stick. He hurled it back over the fence, and shouted in the same direction that he would call the police if there were more trouble. Meanwhile, he told the children to play in the garden with their puppy whenever they wanted and make as much noise as they liked. After a certain timidity, they began playing with Nutmeg again, and 'Meg – Meg – Meg!' resounded as before.

The sponge-cake stayed on the Copley front doorstep until the birds had pecked it into ruin. Mrs Tillotson watched with disappointment and increased misgiving. She hesitated, but at last telephoned Mr Copley's niece. The niece came down a second time to urge Mr Copley to leave. 'But he won't,' she told Mrs Tillotson. She had dropped in to return the cake-plate, and found Mrs Tillotson in the middle of cooking, and Lydia mixing the puppy's tea. 'He won't leave that house; yet he can't bear living there. Everything, every minute of the day, reminds him of Auntie Margaret. Things prey on his mind – drive him crazy. He says he hears voices – voices calling . . .'

When she went, Mr Copley's niece left a spare key to his house. 'Just in case,' she said to Mrs Tillotson. 'I'd be so grateful. In case Uncle gets worse in some way . . .' Rather unwillingly (as Lydia saw), Mrs Tillotson took the key. She put it on the top shelf of the kitchen dresser, out of sight.

In what way could Mr Copley be expected to get worse? There was no more banging or throwing of walking-sticks over the fence, although the children still played outside with Nutmeg, calling to him constantly by name. Lydia paused sometimes to listen by the fence: she was aware of someone treading the paths in the Copley garden next door. Someone who never spoke.

Mrs Tillotson listened to her children playing in the garden and thought of things that Mr Copley's niece had told her – of one thing in particular. Perhaps it was an unimportant thing; perhaps her family would laugh at her for speaking of it. Yet she did speak of it at last, beginning in a rather roundabout way.

'Do you know what the name was – the first name – of poor Mrs Copley?'

They all looked blank, until Lydia said, 'When we were new here, Mrs Copley – she was nice – asked me what my name was, and I said Lydia; and then I asked her what she was called, and I think she said Margaret.'

'Margaret!' said Mr Tillotson. 'Of course, that was it! It was said at the funeral.'

'Yes, Margaret,' said Mrs Tillotson. 'I just wondered if you'd realized: Margaret. All her family – and his family – called her that, except for Mr Copley. His niece told me he had a pet name for her. He always called her Meg.' Mrs Tillotson repeated, 'He always called her Meg.'

'So?' asked Mr Tillotson, as though puzzled; but Lydia thought he knew what her mother was driving at. He must remember, as they all remembered, that name – Meg – being called and shouted over and over again in the Tillotson garden. It would have been heard all over the Copley garden and even in the house of mourning itself.

'So?' Mr Tillotson repeated, angrily this time; but his wife would say no more. Joe and Sam looked confused and rather scared; Lydia was not confused. She stroked Nutmeg and wished that they had given him another name.

Nothing more was said on the subject.

At about this time there must have been a great deal of telephoning between old Mr Copley and his niece. One day the Tillotsons heard that, after all, he had decided to move: he had agreed to live with his niece's family.

So one Sunday morning there was old Mr Copley, white-faced and wild-eyed, waiting at his own front gate with a small suitcase. When his niece's car at last drew up, he bundled himself and his suitcase into it at once. The Tillotsons could see that there was some kind of quite violent argument in the car between uncle and niece, that delayed their departure. In the end, they drove off; and that was the last that the Tillotson family ever saw of old Mr Copley.

Later, on the telephone, the niece explained that Mr Copley had been adamant about leaving the house at once and for good, there and then, and never going back inside it. That was what the argument in the car had been about. Of course, the niece would have to come down again in a week or so to clear the house of its contents and put it up for sale. (That was when she would call on the Tillotsons to reclaim the spare key.)

Meanwhile, the Tillotson family had its own worries: the puppy had disappeared. He had a dog-sized cat-door from the house into the garden, so that he could come and go as he pleased. The garden itself, including the front garden, had been completely dog-proofed against escape. Yet he had gone.

Nutmeg had vanished between their all going to bed – rather late – on Saturday night and their coming down for breakfast on Sunday morning. That was the very Sunday of Mr Copley's going, so, for a short time, suspicion fell on him. 'Mr Copley's stolen our Nutmeg!' Joe had cried. 'He's taken him with him.'

'Don't be ridiculous!' Mrs Tillotson said. 'He got into that car with a suitcase, nothing else.'

'Perhaps Nutmeg was inside the suitcase,' suggested Sam, who seemed to think this possibility would cheer everyone up.

'Alive or dead?' their father inquired sarcastically.

Sam burst into tears; and their mother forbade them to say or think any more about Mr Copley and his suitcase.

One thing was certain: if Nutmeg had not escaped, he must have been taken. That would have been quite easy if the family were not about. For the puppy would always come, wagging his tail, to anyone who appeared at the front gate. A thief had only to lean over and scoop the puppy up.

The Tillotsons told the police of their loss, and put **'Lost'** notices (with mention of **'Reward'**) all around the neighbourhood. But nobody brought news of Nutmeg.

That was on Monday; and by Monday night the Tillotson family were grieving as if for the puppy's death. Mrs Tillotson tried to cheer them: 'He may still be brought back, you know.' Everyone tried to believe that.

Everyone except Lydia. She went to bed without feeling the hope that her mother had suggested, and fell into a blackness of sleep. She did not exactly dream, if dreams are seen. In blackness she saw nothing, only heard voices – Tillotson voices shrieking, 'Meg – Meg – Meg!' and old Mr Copley's frantic voice when he threw the walking-stick, and then

59

another voice, very quiet and calm, that she thought at first was the voice of Mrs Copley talking pleasantly to a little girl. But no – it was not that. It was not a particularly pleasant – or unpleasant – voice: it was just an extraordinarily *close* voice. A voice that seemed to come from inside herself, to be herself. The voice, calm, unhurried, told her that there was no time to be lost. She knew what she had to do.

Lydia woke.

She switched on the light and saw from her clock that there was plenty of time yet before her parents would rouse. She got out of bed and drew back the curtains: outside was dark, but she knew that that was probably the effect of the electric light. She turned out the light and looked again: sure enough, outside was now a grey half-dark that would gradually become the dawn. There was already just enough light outside to see by.

She dressed and crept downstairs. In the kitchen she reached up to the top shelf of the dresser where she had seen her mother hide the Copley front door key, and took it. Very quietly she let herself out of the house, and then out through the Tillotson front gate, and then in through the Copley front gate and up to the Copley front door, and then a turning of the key in the lock and she stepped into the Copley hall.

Here she paused, half-frightened, half-triumphant at what she had already achieved so easily. And what did she mean to do next?

She was going to do what her parents would certainly not have approved of: she would search the house from top to bottom for Nutmeg, and she must begin at once. Ahead of her were the stairs, and she must climb them to search bedroom after bedroom. She would come to the bedroom where Mrs Copley had died: she must search that too.

She had set off across the hall towards the stairs before she noticed the stair-cupboard. Its door stood open, and there was a muddle of something lying on the hall floor that seemed to have come from inside the cupboard. It looked perhaps like *someone* lying there, half inside and half outside the cupboard, and swathed or piled with clothing. That was a horrid idea, so Lydia very quickly and firmly went closer, and there was enough daylight by now to see that the muddle was of clothing only – clothing that came from inside the cupboard.

She peered inside the cupboard.

It was very dark inside, and she wished she had brought a torch with her. But if this stair-cupboard were like their own cupboard – and all the houses were built alike – it had its own electric light. But would the electricity have been cut off by old Mr Copley before he left? She felt up and down just inside the door, where their own light switch would have been. She found a switch, pressed it, and the inside of the cupboard was glaring at her.

Lydia found that she was standing at the foot of a

mountain of clothes – all women's clothes, as far as she could see: blouses and jerseys, and a sparkly party dress that glittered in the bright light, and underwear and tights, and a dressing-gown, and skirts, and high-heeled shoes, and a lacy nightdress, and silk scarves – all piled high in an enormous heap of garments that someone had hurled higgledy-piggledy into this stair-cupboard, not managing to get quite everything in anyway, leaving some half-outside – and then perhaps rushing away.

Surely the only person who could have done this strange thing must have been old Mr Copley himself?

Lydia gazed in wonder, then was about to turn away to begin her proper search, when she heard a tiny sound like a mouse scratching the floor-boards. It came from inside the cupboard.

She stood quite still. Listened.

Dared to hope.

The feeble sound came again. She whispered: 'Meg?' and saw the slightest movement among the clothing towards the edge of the heap.

Then she was on her knees, scrabbling at the pile, burrowing into it, her fingers tangling in folds of clothing and the snares of ribbons and belts. She fought her way through everything until her fingers found something small and warm – and also bony – that moved, although feebly: 'Meg!'

The little dog had been tied by someone with a string to one of the pipes at the back of the stair-cupboard; and then that same someone – old Mr Copley, two days ago – had frenziedly thrown over the puppy all the contents of dead Mrs Copley's wardrobe and chest-of-drawers.

Lydia untied the string and, with both hands round the puppy's body, picked it up gently and cuddled it to her. It still lived. She carried it into the kitchen and ran a teaspoonsful of water into the palm of her hand. She held her hand under the puppy's muzzle, and it licked.

'Darling Nutmeg,' she whispered, 'you're safe now. You're all right now.'

She was beginning to cry, her tears falling on the puppy's head and settling among the hairs of his fur.

She heard, without bothering, the sound of footsteps hesitating at the open front door and then coming into the hall, and then stopping again. 'Lydia?' Her father's voice sounded anxious and at the same time angry.

She could not answer him, but he heard some sound from the kitchen and found her there. Now he was truly furious – until he saw the puppy.

'What on earth –!'

She told him about the stair-cupboard, the burial mound of Mrs Copley's clothes, the string tied to the pipe.

Her father said, 'No – oh, no!' as though he could not bear to believe what he was hearing. He covered his face with his hands.

'But, Dad,' said Lydia, 'Nutmeg's going to be all

right. I'm sure he is. There's no need to tell the police or anything.' She was remembering her father's rage at the time of the thrown walking-stick. 'We can take him to the vet just to make sure he's going to be all right. But he is going to be.'

Her father took his hands from his face, and said: 'Poor, poor creature . . .' At first Lydia thought he meant the puppy, but he went on, always to himself: 'Poor crazy old man . . . poor crazy old creature . . .'

He pulled himself together. 'Come on, Lyddy. Your mum's already worried to death about where you might be. Bring the dog and we'll go home.'

Lydia held the puppy close, and her father put an arm round them both. So they left the Copley house together, locking up behind them as they went.

Only a little later that morning the whole Tillotson family took Nutmeg to the vet. Lydia had been sure that Nutmeg was going to be all right, and the vet confirmed that. He gave them exact instructions on how they should feed him and exercise him: at first, very carefully until he was strong again.

In due course, Mr Copley's niece came to clear the house. (The Tillotsons said nothing about what had happened.) The house was sold to a young couple with a baby, with whom the Tillotsons were immediately on first-name terms. The baby would love playing with Nutmeg when it was older.

Nutmeg kept his full name, but Mr Tillotson did not want him to be called Meg any more. He forbade it. He would not discuss his reasons, and Mrs Tillotson stayed out of any argument.

So the puppy's name was shortened in the opposite direction, to Nuts, or Nutter, or Nutty. This was confusing for the puppy at first, but he soon got used to his new name. And, after all, as Lydia said, the new name suited him very well. He was a little dog easily excited to madness, barking at the top of his voice, quite crazy with the joy of being alive.

# Bluebag

My great-aunt – Aunt Carrie – simply loved our washing-machine. She'd sit by it while it hummed and thundered, and tell stories of her youth, when there weren't such things. In those days there were huge coppers for boiling clothes and tubs for lesser washes and also dollies and mangles and great bars of yellow soap and bluebag.

The story of bluebag and Spot was one of my Aunt Carrie's favourites. Spot had been her dog when she was a girl, and bluebag – well, it almost describes itself. It was the size of a very large lump of sugar, solid blue, and you bought it tied up in a white cotton rag. It was dipped into the water when white things were being washed: the blueness seeped out into the water, and so the white things washed whiter. Aunt Carrie's mother always kept bluebag for laundry-work, and for a second purpose, 'to which' (my Aunt Carrie liked mysteriously to say) 'I will come later in my story.'

One sunny summer's day, long ago, Aunt Carrie was at a loose end. She looked thoughtfully at Spot, who was one of those dogs mostly white but with a few spots of brown and black. He was a small dog, and usually very fond of my Aunt Carrie.

My aunt addressed him: 'Now, Spot, you'd like to be nice and clean and white and fluffy, wouldn't you? Of course you would!'

If Spot could have spoken, he would have answered, 'Carrie, *no*!'

He disliked water, except for drinking. He was suspicious even of the fish-pond at the bottom of the garden, and that was what a dog might call *natural* water, clear at the top and deep mud at the bottom, where the water weeds rooted themselves. As for a large quantity of clean tap-water gently steaming in an old tin bath out on the lawn – that horrified him. He knew what it meant.

And that was exactly what my aunt Carrie had in mind. She chose the longest dog-lead, clipped it to Spot's collar and then tied the other end to an apple tree on the edge of the lawn. Escape for Spot became impossible.

My Aunt Carrie fetched the tin bath and filled it

with warm water, transported in jug after jug from the house. Spot sat and watched her. His ears drooped.

She fetched the soap and a scrubbing-brush; also the bluebag. My aunt's reasoning was that people used bluebag to wash white clothes whiter; so why not use it in washing Spot?

The sun was hot, but it's always best to give a dog a brisk rubbing down immediately after a bath. My aunt needed some kind of towel. Her mother was fussy about the family towels, so her father, who occasionally washed Spot if he were muddy or smelly, always made do with a clean sack. There were plenty of those, my aunt said. Her father used them in the apple-room in the old part of the house: in winter, he spread them over the harvested apples to keep the frost off. As the family ate its way through the apples, the sacks were taken up, one by one, shaken, folded loosely, and stored on top of each other in a neat pile.

So Aunt Carrie went along to the apple-room to fetch a sack. By now, of course, all the apples were eaten and the apple-room was empty except for the mound of sacks in one corner. The room, so cold in winter, was now stuffily hot. The one window had jammed shut long ago, and the only ventilation was through a broken pane of glass. A wasp – obviously the apple-room was a pleasant place for them, even empty – sailed out through the hole as Aunt Carrie was looking, and another sailed in.

The topmost sack of the pile looked newish and

clean, but – to be on the safe side – my Aunt Carrie decided to shake it to get rid of any leafy, apple-stalk dust there might be. She took a good grip of the sack, yanked it off the pile and, with the same movement, gave it a quick, strong shake.

At this point my Aunt Carrie, who prided herself on her grasp of *suspense* in storytelling, would pause to ask –

How long does it take to give a quick, strong shake to a folded sack?

One second?

Two seconds? Perhaps three?

For one of those seconds she had turned her head away, to avoid getting any apple-dust into her eyes. But something warned her – there was something odd, perhaps, in the *feel* of the sack – even before the end of that second. She turned her head quickly to look, and – even as she looked – flung the sack from her.

For the shaking open of the folded sack had in one instant both shown and shattered a *thing* that had been built within the concealment of the folds – a rounded, dun-coloured structure about the size of a child's head. As the sack shot from her fingers across the apple-room, torn pieces of papery walls and roofings broke from it, and in the ruined chambers and passageways she glimpsed living things no longer than her thumbnail – some smaller – moving and squirming and crawling. And some had wings and began to fly . . .

Yellow and black-barred, they began to fly, and she

knew them. Wasps and wasps and more wasps – more and more wasps than she had ever seen together before in her whole life.

Never before or since (said my aunt in a kind of horrified wonder) had she seen a *lived-in* wasps' nest so close, so open to her inspection; and she hoped never to see one so again. Within the seconds of revelation the sack went flying, she went flying, and the wasps came flying after her. Before she was fairly out of the apple-room – and she was moving fast, *fast* – two or three of the quicker-witted wasps had caught up with her and stung her. She was wearing only a sleeveless dress and her legs were bare, so it was easy for them.

My aunt was running at top speed, with amazing acceleration from standstill, but wasps seemed to catch up with her (she said) quite effortlessly. She tore from the apple-room down the passage to the main part of the house. She must have been shrieking, for she could already hear Spot in the distance barking in a frenzy of reply. Her family roused to the alarm, of course. But she was down the stairs and through the hall so fast that she never saw her father. Apparently he had stepped forward towards my Aunt Carrie in her flight, then noticed the wasps hot in her pursuit, and, with great common sense, as my aunt admitted, drew back. Apparently he had shouted to her to make for the fish-pond, but my aunt never heard him.

My Aunt Carrie tore down the hall, through the open garden door, and out on to the lawn. There was the tin tub and the yellow soap and the bluebag that, hundreds of years before it seemed, she had intended using; and there was Spot jumping about at the end of his lead and barking so continuously and shrilly that he was almost screaming, too. He had – again with great good sense – rushed to the furthest extent of his lead, well clear of the route that the wasps were taking.

Meanwhile, my aunt never stopped running. Across the lawn and down the length of the garden and the orchard, and suddenly there was the fish-pond. My aunt ran straight off the ground and into the water.

Into the water and down – down – so that the water closed over her head, and my aunt said she could have laughed for joy, except that you don't laugh under water. When she came up, there were a few wasps trying to swim – they must have floated off her clothes and hair and skin – and a good many others were flying around, much taken aback.

My aunt thought it wise to submerge again at once. She did so again and again and again. At the last coming up to snatch air, she observed that there were no more wasps hanging around on the off chance (as she put it). In the distance they could be seen straggling home-ward, disgruntled.

My Aunt Carrie crawled out of the fish-pond. From the top of her head downwards she was covered with mud and water-weed. She staggered to her feet and began squelchily to walk back to the house. She was careful not to catch up with any wasps as she went.

Her mother came hurrying – but, equally, on a *careful* route – to meet her. When she saw the state my aunt was in, she turned back, crying that she would start to run a bath for her at once. In the mean time her father was preparing to untie Spot from his tree and tidy away the tin bath, the scrubbing-brush, the soap and the bluebag. He paused as my aunt drew level with him. He said, 'You'll need this, my girl,' and handed her the bluebag.

At this point in her story my Aunt Carrie became triumphant. Above the roar of the washing-machine, she would shout, 'I said I'd let you into the secret of the bluebag – its second use. You don't know? You haven't guessed? In those days bluebag was used against bites and stings. My mother always dabbed it, wet, on a wasp-sting to soothe the pain and the swelling.

'So, after my bath, there was I with runny blue blotches all over my face and arms and legs. My little dog came to see me, and my father – who always thought he had a great sense of humour – said he couldn't tell us apart for the spots. He called us Spot the Dog and Spot the Daughter.'

My Aunt Carrie would laugh heartily; then sometimes would add thoughtfully: 'But I remember that it didn't seem funny at the time.'

# Mrs Chamberlain's
# Reunion

This is a tale of long ago. I was a little boy, and our family lived – no, *resided* – among other well-off families in a Residential Neighbourhood. All those neighbours were people like ourselves, who thought well of themselves and also liked to keep themselves to themselves.

Except for one neighbour. That's where my story starts.

On one side of us had lived for many years the Miss Hardys, two spinster sisters, very ladylike. Our two gardens were separated by a trellis fence with rambler roses, a rather sketchy, see-through affair. So our family had at least an acquaintance with the Miss Hardys, and my sister, Celia, knew them quite well. As a little girl she had played with their cat, Mildred, until it died of old age.

Of course, we had neighbours on the other side, too; but on that side a thick laurel hedge grew so high that these neighbours – to us children, anyway – seemed hardly to exist.

In all the years that we lived in our house (and it had been bought by my father from a family called Chamberlain, just before my birth), neighbours may have come and gone beyond the laurel hedge, but we never noticed.

Then one day there was a new neighbour and suddenly things were different. The new neighbour cut down the hedge – not to the ground of course but to shoulder level. He thus revealed himself to us: Mr Wilfred Brown, retired and a widower.

He was a well-built man with a pointed, inquisitive nose. His eyes, large and prominent, looked glancingly, missing nothing; yet his gaze could settle with close attention. My mother said he stared.

My mother snubbed Mr Brown's attempts at conversation over what remained of the hedge. She had decided that he was what she called 'common'. She remarked to my father that Mr Brown had been a *butcher* – and my father, in rare joking mood, pointed out that he had indeed butchered the hedge. But my father was no more ready than my mother for a friendly chat with Mr Brown.

We three children, however, had been strictly taught to be attentive and polite to our elders. In the garden, therefore, we were at Mr Brown's mercy. He hailed us, talked with us, questioned us. We had to answer. Thus Mr Brown discovered that, in our well-ordered family way, we would be off on our fortnight's summer holiday, starting – as always – on the second Saturday of August.

The date was then the thirtieth of July.

The next time that my mother went into the garden, to cut flowers for an arrangement, Mr Brown accosted her over the hedge. He begged to be allowed 'to keep a friendly and watchful eye' on our house while we were away at the seaside.

My mother answered with instant refrigeration: '*Too* kind, Mr Brown! But we could not possibly put you to such trouble. We shall make our usual arrangements.'

Mr Brown asked, 'How good are these arrangements, Mrs Carew? What are they exactly?' He gazed earnestly, and the point of his nose seemed to quiver.

My mother was flustered by Mr Brown's stare. She was forced into explaining in detail that the Miss Hardys would be left with the key to the house, as well as with our telephone number at the seaside. But all this was only for use in case of emergency.

Mr Brown shook his head. 'The Miss Hardys, you

say? Oh, dear me! Ladies are prone to panic in an emergency.'

By now my mother had recovered herself. She retorted quite sharply: 'The Miss Hardys are never prone to anything, Mr Brown.'

Mr Brown smiled and shook his head again. So there the matter was left. My mother could hardly forbid a neighbour to focus his eyes sometimes on our house, now so very visible over the low hedge. So, for the first time since we had lived there, our empty house would be overlooked not only by the Miss Hardys, but also by our new neighbour on the other side, Mr Brown.

Meanwhile, that second Saturday in August was drawing nearer and nearer.

I was the youngest child and excited at the thought of the sea and the seaside. The other two were much calmer; they remembered so well other fortnights beginning with that second Saturday in August. Celia told me privately that Robert, the eldest of us, had said (but not in our parents' hearing, of course) that family holidays got duller and duller.

Celia herself would probably be too preoccupied with her white mouse, Micky, to be bored on the holiday. There was nothing at all remarkable about Micky, except that neither of our parents knew of his existence. They had never liked animals. They hadn't really approved of Celia's playing with the Hardys' cat; they were relieved when Mildred died.

Disappointingly for Celia, the Hardys did not get another cat — Mildred had only been inherited from their old friend and neighbour, Mrs Chamberlain, when she died. Celia missed a pet, and at last — most daringly and, of course, secretly — had acquired Micky. She would take Micky on holiday with her, and his very private companionship would console her during her seaside fortnight.

At the seaside we always stayed in the same guest-house and did the same things — that was one of Robert's complaints. My father played golf and did some sea-fishing; and, whatever the weather, he swam every morning before breakfast, taking Robert with him. Sometimes he shared with my mother the duty of supervising our play: we were allowed to paddle and trawl in rock-pools with nets and to make sand-castles and sand-pictures. Sometimes we went for long walks inland, all five of us. Of course, there were wet Augusts, but my father never allowed rain to keep us indoors for even half a day. One could walk quite well in mackintoshes and Wellington boots, he said; and our landlady, Mrs Prothero, was obliging about the drying out of wet clothes.

Our return from these holidays was always the same. As the car turned into our quiet, tree-lined street, there was our house, but first my mother had to collect the key from the Miss Hardys.

'All has been well, I hope, Miss Hardy?'

'Nothing at all for you to worry about, Mrs Carew.'

The younger Miss Hardy, from behind her sister in the doorway, would ask, 'And you had a restful holiday, Mrs Carew?'

'Restful and delightful,' said my mother. 'Perhaps a little rainy, but that never kept us indoors. And now it's good to be home.'

Having recovered the key from the Miss Hardys, my mother would rejoin the family as we waited at our own front door. She handed the key to my father. He unlocked the door, and we entered. We brought with us the salty smell of the seaside rising from our hair and skin and clothing and from the collections of seashore pebbles and shells in our buckets. That saltiness, together with fresh air from newly opened windows, soon began to get rid of the stuffy, rather unpleasant smell of an empty house shut up for a whole fortnight. Soon our home was exactly as it had always been; and so it would remain for another year, until another second Saturday in August.

But this particular year our seaside holiday could not possibly have been described as restful and delightful, even by my mother; and our home-coming was to be very different.

From that second Saturday in August rain fell without stopping: this we had had to endure on holidays before now. What was new was Robert's sullen ill-temper, as continuous as the rain and as damping. He said nothing openly, for my father could be very sharp with a child of his ungrateful enough not to enjoy the

78

holiday he was providing. My mother tried to soothe and smooth. She gave out that Robert was probably incubating some mild infection.

As if to prove her point, Robert developed a heavy cold after one of our wet walks and sneezed all over Mrs Prothero's paying guests' sitting-room. He had to borrow his father's linen handkerchiefs, and Mrs Prothero had to boil them after use, and dry them and iron them. Mrs Prothero complained about the extra work; and we all caught Robert's cold. In spite of this, my father continued to play golf and to fish, until one morning he embedded a fish-hook in the palm of his right hand. He came out of the local hospital with his hand bandaged, and in a bad temper. No more golf or fishing for the rest of the holiday.

This all happened in our first week. We were still, however, expecting to remain at the seaside, enjoying ourselves, to the end of our fortnight.

Then came the telephone call.

We had returned from a moist morning's walk to be told that a Mr Wilfred Brown had telephoned. He had urgently asked that Mr or Mrs Carew should telephone him back as soon as possible.

'What's the man on about?' my father demanded fretfully. 'Telephone him back, indeed! Does he think I'm made of money?'

'Perhaps something's wrong at home,' faltered my mother. She was remembering Mr Brown's 'watchful eye'.

'Rubbish!' said my father. 'One of the Miss Hardys would have telephoned us; not this Brown fellow.'

He was so enraged with Mr Brown that when, during lunch, the telephone rang again for Mr or Mrs Carew, my mother had to deal with it. She went most reluctantly; she returned clearly shaken. 'Mr Brown was surprised that we hadn't rung back.' (My father snorted.) 'He thinks there's something wrong at home. He's been on the watch and he's sure there are goings on (as he puts it) inside our house. He's sure that "something's up".'

'Inside our house!' cried my father, throwing aside his napkin. 'Then why on earth hasn't the fool got the police? Burglars! – and he just . . . Oh, the idiot, the juggins!'

'No,' said my mother. 'Nobody's broken in; he was quite positive about that. This is different, he says. Something wrong *inside the house*.'

My father stared in angry disbelief. Then he gave his orders. 'Go and telephone the Miss Hardys.' (My father felt that, as a general rule, ladies should communicate with ladies; men with men.) 'Tell them what Brown says, and find out – oh! just find out *something*!'

My father bade us all go on with our lunch, as he himself did; and my mother went to the telephone again. She came back after a while, still troubled. 'I told them, dear, and they're sure there's nothing at all for us to worry about. They insist that's so. But they're upset by Mr Brown's suspicions. I didn't tell you at the

80

time, dear, but he asked me on the telephone whether we'd empowered – that was his word: *empowered* – the Miss Hardys to use the house in our absence. But they say they've never set foot over the threshold in our absence. Ever. It's all rather strange and horrid . . .'

We three children listened, appalled – delightfully appalled. If the Miss Hardys were other than they had always seemed – if they were liars, trespassers, thieves – if all this, then houses might come toppling about our ears and cars take off with wings.

My father had risen from his carving chair. 'There's only one thing to be done: we go home. Now. At once. We catch them red-handed.'

'Red-handed?' my mother repeated faintly, thinking no doubt of the towering respectability of the two Miss Hardys; and, 'Now? When we're only half-way through our holiday?'

'Damn the holiday!' cried my father, who never swore in the presence of his family. 'We're going home. There are hours yet of daylight. If we leave now, we can be there before dark. Everyone pack at once.'

There was trouble with Mrs Prothero. At the time several of my father's handkerchiefs were simmering away soapily in one of her saucepans. Also my father thought that the holiday charge should be reduced by more than Mrs Prothero would agree to.

However, within the hour, ourselves and our belongings (including, of course, Celia's stowaway mouse) were packed into the car; Mrs Prothero's account had been settled ('Shark!' said my father); and we were off. For once, my mother drove, as my father's injured hand would not allow him to.

Of course, Mr Brown, having been at such pains to warn us, must have been on the lookout for our return. And if my father had hoped to catch the Miss Hardys unawares (let alone 'red-handed'), he under-estimated the alertness of elderly maiden ladies. We drove up under darkened skies and pouring rain, and my mother was about to get out of the car, when the Miss Hardys, together under a huge umbrella, rushed down their front path to greet us.

My father had lowered the window on the passen-ger side and now called sternly, 'Good evening. We need our front-door key, please.'

Unmistakably the Miss Hardys were taken aback by our arrival – indeed, they seemed the very picture of guilt caught red-handed. 'Oh, dear!' and 'Oh, no!' they cried desperately. 'So early back from your holi-day!' and, 'Surely you won't want to go into your house now, at once? Surely not! Oh, dear! Oh, dear!'

'The key!' said my father, and got it.

Quite a large party gathered in the shelter of our porch: my father in front with the key; the rest of his family behind him; behind us, again, the two Miss Hardys, still distraught; and behind them – although at first we were unaware of his having joined us – Mr Wilfred Brown.

My father, left-handed but resolute, inserted the

key in the lock, turned it and pushed open the front door.

We had been expecting to enter or at least to peer forward, even if fearfully, into the hall. Instead, we found ourselves reeling back from a smell – a *stench* – which flowed out towards us. We knew when the tide had reached the last of our party because 'Phew! What a stinker!' exclaimed Mr Brown, thus declaring his presence through a handkerchief muffling nose and mouth.

But, in spite of the smell, we could, of course, see into the hall. (Surely my father saw *something*, however much he afterwards preferred to deny that?) To me the hall seemed somehow darker than one would expect, even on an evening so overcast – darker in the way of having more shadows to it; and the shadows seemed to shift and flicker and move. They were just above ground level.

And I was almost sure that – for a moment only – I glimpsed a taller shadow whose shape I could interpret: it was human, and surely female. I was not alone in this perception. The Miss Hardys had edged forward, and one now whispered, 'Yes, it *is* dear Mrs Chamberlain!' and the other, clearly in an agony of social embarrassment, murmured: 'We are in the wrong. We are intruding upon the privacy of dear Mrs Chamberlain's reunion!'

And then the shadowy figure had vanished.

Even before the Miss Hardys' whispering, I was

aware that Celia was standing on tiptoe for a better view into the hall. With the keen eye of love, she recognized – or thought she recognized – one shape among the low-moving shadows. She became certain: 'Mildred!' she cried. She took three eager steps past my father and across the threshold of the front door into the hall itself.

There she was halted abruptly by the behaviour of someone whom, in the excitement, she had quite forgotten: her dear Micky. Up to now he had been in the concealment and safety of a pocket.

If the extraordinary smell from the house was sickening for us, it must have crazed with fear the poor mouse. He attempted to escape.

His small white face was already visible over the edge of Celia's pocket; and it was as if the shadowy house saw him. (If walls have ears, why not eyes, too? Eyes that stare, that glare, that stupefy.)

I suppose that – if he were capable of planning at all – Micky must have meant to leap from Celia's pocket and instantly leave the house at greatest speed by the open front door. But the gaze of the shadowy hall was full upon him: he did not leap, but fell helplessly from Celia's pocket on to the floor of the hall and lay there motionless.

('Oh!' moaned my mother, and there was a small clatter as she fainted away in her corner of the porch among the potted plants. She knew how a lady should react to the sight of a mouse.)

What followed is difficult to describe. It was as if the house – not the bricks and mortar, of course, but the inside of the house, the shadowy air itself – gathered together swiftly and with one ferocious purpose against a terrified white mouse –

– And pounced!

Micky gave one heart-rending squeak – a mouse-shriek that rose to heaven imploring mercy, and met none. He died in mid-squeak; and Celia fell on her knees by his body, babbling grief.

And the last of the slinking shadows melted away, every last one of them.

Only the smell remained; and later my intelligent nose would remember and make a connection between the present appalling stench of cat and the peculiar and rather repellent stuffiness of our house after every seaside holiday. In that stuffiness lurked the very last faint trace of this present horror of a smell.

As for my father, he would never, anyway, countenance any idea of the supernatural: he had always ridiculed it. The very idea of *evidence* put him into a fury. Now he was beside himself with indignation. 'What is going on?' he shouted into the empty hall.

There was no reply – no sound at all except a slight scuffling from the back of the porch, where my mother was beginning to struggle among the potted plants; also Celia's quiet sobbing. He picked on that. He realized that the mouse had been Celia's rash secret. In this she had been, he said, deceitful, disobedient and – oh, yes!

defiant and disloyal. Under the fury of her father's attack, Celia's weeping became hysterical. Her tears rained down upon the corpse clasped to her breast, and she was led away by the Miss Hardys to be given sal volatile and sympathy.

My father now turned to the plight of my mother in her porch corner. On regaining consciousness, she had opened her eyes to find Mr Brown's gazing fully into them at a distance of about three and a half inches. And he was now gallantly assisting her with helping hands, one at her waist, another at her elbow. My father rushed down upon them, demanding that Mr Brown remove himself instantly from his wife and his porch and the rest of his property. Without pause he went on to attack Mr Brown's birth, breeding, appearance, character and former occupation – '*trade*'! (Rage always inspired my father.)

Mr Brown was neither foolhardy nor a fool. He retreated. Out into the drenching rain he went, and home. We all watched him go. That was really the last we saw of Mr Brown. Within two days my father had caused a seven-foot-high solid fence to be built just our side of the laurel hedge.

Having dispatched Mr Brown, my father became master again in his own house. He instructed us to go round opening all the windows to let what he called 'this stale air' out and the fresh air in. Never mind the rain. Then we must unpack. 'Our holiday is over; we are at home; we resume our routine.'

In the long term, however, our routine had been undermined; and for this my father could not forgive the Miss Hardys. He suspected them of conniving at happenings which were all the more deplorable because they simply could not have occurred. He had known of the existence of the late Mrs Chamberlain, of course, because he had bought our house from her heirs. He may even have heard of her mania for cats. ('She couldn't resist a stray,' the Miss Hardys explained to Celia. 'She tried to keep the numbers down. But, by the end – well, the house did begin rather to *smell*. Cats, you know . . .')

My father would never admit to what became obvious: that the ghosts of Mrs Chamberlain and her cats had been returning regularly to haunts where they had been happy. They had been tempted by the absolute regularity of our holiday absences to hold a kind of annual Old Girls' Reunion in our house – but there must have been Old Boys as well. Only the attendance of at least one tom-cat could explain the strength of that smell.

The Miss Hardys had known what was going on every August, but saw no harm in it. The ghosts came promptly after our departure for the seaside, and had always vacated the house well before the date of our return. 'It was all so discreetly done!' the Miss Hardys remarked plaintively to Celia, as they administered the sal volatile. 'Such a pity that it should have to stop!'

But it did. Before the next summer, we had moved

house; and I do not suppose that any family succeeding us could have had such a very dependable holiday routine. I only hope the ghosts were not too much disappointed.

After that summer my father became – and remained – jumpy about family holidays. We were never allowed to go at the same time for two years running. This meant, incidentally, that we no longer stayed in Mrs Prothero's guest-house. In a huff she had said that she could not be expected to be 'irregularly available'.

The Miss Hardys were seldom spoken of; Mr Brown never.

# The Nest Egg

School was dreary for William Penney. He was no good there. He was no good at lessons, or at games, and he was no good at making new friends. Teachers, privately warned to make allowances for him, found him difficult in a dull way. His worst stroke of luck turned out to be his name. Nothing wrong with William, you might think; but another – and better-liked – boy in the class had the same name. Everybody said he had first claim to it, since William Penney was the newcomer. So what was William Penney to be called?

Someone, with a snigger, suggested Willy; and then everybody sniggered. William did not mind much; as long as they left him alone, he could bear sniggerings.

But then someone said, 'Well, he's got a second name, hasn't he? W. H. Penney – he wrote his name once like that. I saw it. Come on, Willy! If you don't want to be called Willy, what does H stand for?'

'I don't mind being called Willy,' said William.

'What does H stand for?'

'It's just my father's name.'

'Well, what *is* your father's name?'

He didn't want to tell them. He didn't want them to know his father's name, because his father was all he had now, and even he was away somewhere. His mother had died.

'I'd rather be called Willy, please.'

But now they knew he did not want to tell them, they tormented him. 'Come on, what is it? Is it Hugh? Or Hubert? Or Herbert? –'

'Or Halibut!' suggested a wit; and the same boy went on, 'Or is it Halgernon? Or Hebenezer? –'

So, after all, he was trapped by his own anger into telling them. Stammering in anger and haste, he cried, 'It's not a stupid name – it's not! It's just Hen – Hen –'

Then they shouted with joyous laughter and called him Hen-Hen-Henny-penny and clucked at him and asked him what he had had for breakfast, and before he had time to answer, answered for him: 'A hegg!'

If they had only known, their teasing came near the truth. William Henry Penney really did have an egg for breakfast, whether he liked it or not, nearly every day of the week, because now he was living with his Aunt Rosa, who kept hens. She ran her garden – almost as big as a small-holding – as a business. She grew all the usual outdoor vegetables, and had a green-house for cucumbers and early tomatoes. At the bottom of the garden and in the orchard, she kept hens; not very many, but good layers. William helped with the hens, feeding them in the morning before he went to school, filling their drinking-bowl with fresh water, and letting them out of their run to roam in his aunt's orchard. He also collected the eggs in the even-ing, but this was only under Aunt Rosa's supervision. He had once broken an egg.

Until now Aunt Rosa had lived by herself, with her dog, Bessy. Aunt Rosa was middle-aged and sharp; Bessy was old and cantankerous. Neither of them was used to having children about the place.

When William's father had brought him here, he explained to his son that this was only until he could find another job in another place, and a new home for them both. 'Until then Rosa has said she'll put up with you – I mean, put you up. Very kind of Rosa,' said William's father. He did not usually think his sister was particularly kind.

'Why's she wearing that scarf of Mum's?' asked William.

His father frowned. He said, 'She's being very help-ful in a bad time, and she asked if she could have it. It was one of the things she wanted.'

'I don't like her having things,' said William.

'Oh, come on, William!' his father said angrily. But William was not deceived: really, his father was angry with Aunt Rosa for wanting things that had so recently belonged to her dead sister-in-law, his own wife, William's mother. He was also angry with himself for having to give in to her.

William's father saw William settled in Aunt Rosa's house. Then he said goodbye, leaving William with Aunt Rosa and Bessy.

In Aunt Rosa's house William had a bedroom to himself, but it was big and bare and lonely after his own old room crammed with his ancient toys and his collections and gadgets and oddments, all in a friendly muddle. He could not feel at home here, in Aunt Rosa's house. Deliberately, he did not unpack his suitcase into the drawers left empty for him.

Nowadays William was always watched; he knew that. In Aunt Rosa's house he was watched by Aunt Rosa and by Bessy, in case he did anything silly, wasteful, or damaging. At school he was watched by those whose fun was to tease him. His only really safe and private time was in bed, at night. Every night he cried himself to sleep – but quietly, so that Aunt Rosa should not hear him and despise him for crying. He had sad dreams that woke him to real sadness. Then he cried for his father, who was far away, and for his mother, who was dead.

One day, in the early evening, Aunt Rosa came

down from her bedroom dressed with unusual care. Besides her good clothes, she was wearing a thin gold chain: William recognized it at once. He had saved up to buy it for his mother on her last birthday.

He couldn't help himself: he said, 'That's my mum's gold chain.'

'Yes,' said his aunt. 'It was hers. It's not real gold, of course. I wouldn't have taken anything valuable from your father, when he pressed me to choose, after the funeral. The chain's not worth anything – just rubbish. But it does for the odd occasion.'

William said nothing aloud, but to himself he said, 'I hate Aunt Rosa. I hate having to live in her house.'

His aunt was dressed up to attend a parish meeting. Before she left, she said to William, 'You should be able to help more on your own by now. Go down to the hen-house and see if there are any eggs. Probably not; the hens are all going off lay. But, if there is an egg, for goodness' sake don't break it! And don't bring out the nest egg, as you did last time!' The nest egg was only an imitation egg: it was left in a nest to encourage the hen to lay other eggs there and nowhere else.

Aunt Rosa went off on her bicycle; Bessy settled herself in her basket in the kitchen; and William went down the garden to the hen-house.

He was still thinking of his mother's gold chain. Of course, he had known that it wasn't made of real gold; but his mother had loved to wear it. He remembered buying it, and keeping it a secret until her birthday. In secret he had played with it, and he could still remember the way the thin links had poured and poured between his fingers. He remembered the way his mother had looked when she wore it; and now he hated to remember how it had looked round the neck of his Aunt Rosa.

Still thinking of the gold chain, he reached the hen-house.

The hen-house was a low, wooden, home-made affair, very simple and rather ramshackle. It had a door at the back, through which the egg-collector could reach in. At the front was a pop-hole through which the hens and the cockerel went out into the run. The run had high chicken-wire walls and a chicken-wire door that let into the orchard. The door was open, as usual in the summer daytime: William had already seen the cockerel and his hens pecking about in the grass of the orchard.

He unlatched the hen-house door and peered in. It was always dim inside the hen-house; but there was not much to see, anyway. Just an earth floor with straw over it, in which the hens hollowed their nests; a perch across from side to side, for the fowls to roost on at night; and the daylight coming in through the pop-hole on the opposite side of the hen-house.

For the first time, William was here without Aunt Rosa nagging him to hurry. He let his eyes accustom themselves to the twilight of the hen-house; and then he saw the eye watching him. It belonged to the one hen that, after all, had not gone out with the others into the orchard. She was crouching in a corner of the hen-house, deep in the straw, absolutely still, absolutely quiet, staring at him.

The hen-house was not large, but it was quite big enough for a boy of William's size to creep inside. He did so now, for the convenience of looking more thoroughly for any eggs. But he kept away from the hen sitting in her corner.

The hen-house smelled of hens – there was a line of hen-droppings in the straw under the perch: the straw would need changing soon. There was also the smell, brought out by the summer heat, of creosote in the wood. All the same, William rather liked being in the hen-house. It was a real house, in its way, and it was just his size. It fitted him; he felt at home in it.

Being careful where he put his feet down in the straw, he searched for eggs. But, as his aunt had prophesied, there were none.

His search brought him to the sitting hen. Surely she must be sitting on something? As he had seen his aunt do, he slid his hand underneath her body to feel for any eggs; but at once she began to fluster and flounder and squawk. Her cries were immediately heard and answered from the orchard by the cockerel, who came running at a great pace and so appeared within seconds at the pop-hole, confronting William with furious enmity.

Once, recently, Aunt Rosa had remarked in scorn

that William couldn't possibly be afraid of an ordinary *cockerel*; but Aunt Rosa was ignorant of a great many of life's possibilities. In this present emergency, William withdrew from the hen-house very quickly indeed, latching the door shut behind him. He heard the cockerel and the hen conferring crossly inside.

Meanwhile, William had an egg in his hand – the only egg that had been under the hen. He opened his hand, and – it was the nest egg, after all! A good thing that Aunt Rosa was not with him! By himself, he had time to look at the nest egg properly. It was made of earthenware, almost as smooth-surfaced as a real egg, and the same size and weight as a real egg. There were differences: the stamp of the maker's name made an unevenness of surface in one place; and there was an air-hole in the side, about the size of a hole down a drinking-straw. And the nest egg was hollow.

William handled the nest egg. He liked it, as he had liked being inside the hen-house. He liked the innocent trickery of it; he liked the neat little hole in its side, that was also the entry to its hollow interior. And, as he studied the nest egg, an idea began to grow in his mind . . .

He pocketed the nest egg and went back indoors. The kitchen door was open and Bessy watched him suspiciously from her basket, but she could see nothing wrong that he was doing. He went upstairs and into his bedroom, and shut the door. He took the nest egg from his pocket and hid it at the bottom of his suitcase.

He was in bed, waiting for sleep, when his aunt came back from her meeting. He heard her lock up, see to Bessy, and then come upstairs to her bedroom. Bessy came with her, because she slept at the foot of her bed at night. Aunt Rosa, with Bessy, went into the bedroom, and the door was shut behind them.

Now Aunt Rosa would be getting ready for bed. She would take her best coat off and hang it in the wardrobe. She would take her shoes off. She would take her dress off – but no! before she did that, she would take off William's gold chain. She took it off and – well, where did she put it? Had she a jewel-box for necklaces and brooches? Or did she put them into some special drawer? Or did she leave them on top of her dressing-table, at least for the time being?

Worrying at uncertainties, William fell into an uneasy sleep. He dreamed sad dreams, as usual; and the saddest – and the silliest, too – was that the nest egg had grown little chicken legs and climbed out of his suitcase and was running to catch his mother's gold chain to eat it, as though it were a worm. But the nest egg never caught up with the gold chain.

The next morning William was woken by his aunt's calling from downstairs: his breakfast was ready. He dressed quickly and then went straight from his bedroom to his aunt's room. Her door was open, and even from the doorway he could see that his mother's gold chain lay coiled on the top of his aunt's dressing-table.

Oh! he was in luck! He had only to cross the bedroom floor and pick up the chain, and it would be his.

He took one step inside the bedroom doorway, and – he was out of luck, after all. He had forgotten that Bessy slept in his aunt's room every night; and here she still was. She lay at the foot of the bed, watching him; and, as he made that quick, furtive movement to enter the bedroom, Bessy growled. He knew that, if he went any further, she would begin to bark – to shout to Aunt Rosa the alarm: 'Thief! Thief!'

He was bitterly disappointed, but he had no choice but to withdraw and go on downstairs. Just as usual he had his breakfast and then fed and watered the fowls and let them out of their run. When he got to school, just as usual, the boys called him Henny-penny and enjoyed their joke. The witty boy of the class sacrificed a small chocolate-and-marshmallow egg by putting it on William's chair just before he sat down. School was hateful to William – as hateful as Aunt Rosa's house.

After school, Aunt Rosa had Willam's tea ready for him.

'I'll just wash my hands upstairs in the bathroom,' he said.

'No, you can do it at the kitchen sink. And, after your tea, I've a job for you.'

And, after his tea, she said, 'Today you can change the straw in the hen-house for me.'

'Now?'

'Yes, now!'

'Shouldn't I go and change out of my school clothes first?' asked William.

Aunt Rosa stared at him suspiciously. 'You're not usually so fussy . . .'

William waited.

'All right then,' said his aunt. 'Change, but be quick about it. I'll be getting you the barrow and the shovel out of the shed.'

She went into the garden, followed by Bessy; and William went swiftly upstairs. The door of his aunt's room was shut, but he opened it without hesitation. He knew he was safe, for he could hear the rattle of the wheelbarrow down the garden as his aunt manoeuvred it out of the shed; and Bessy would be there with her, too.

The gold chain had not been put away: it lay just as before on the top of the dressing-table. He felt like crying as he picked it up: he had so longed to have it.

He disturbed nothing else, and shut his aunt's bed-room door as he left. Then he went on to his own room. One hand held the gold chain – he would not put it down for an instant; with the other hand he burrowed into his suitcase and brought out the nest egg. He turned the egg so that its air-hole was upper-most. Then, with the fingers of his other hand, he found the free end of the gold chain, and held it exactly above the air-hole. He began to lower it towards the air-hole, to feed it through; and it went through! He had foreseen correctly: the size was right.

He went on dropping the gold chain, link by link, through the air-hole of the nest egg. The links fell and fell and fell until there were no more; and the whole chain had disappeared inside the nest egg; and still the egg was not full. He shook the nest egg, and he could hear the supple chain shifting and settling inside its new home.

'William!' his aunt shouted from the garden. He put the nest egg into his pocket and then had to take it out again, because he had forgotten that he was supposed to be changing into rough clothes. He changed quickly and, with the nest egg in a pocket, went down to the job in the hen-house. 'For goodness' sake, boy!' said his aunt. 'I thought you were never coming! Here's the barrow and shovel. Clean the shed right out and barrow the soiled straw to the compost heap. Then fresh straw from the shed. I want to see the job well done. Oh! – and mind the nest egg!'

She left him to his work. The re-strawing took some time, but William did well. His aunt had grudgingly to admit that, when she inspected the inside of the hen-house. She also noted the presence of the nest egg, just where it should be.

And William left it there.

Aunt Rosa's discovery of the loss of the gold chain was not made until the following morning. William was woken by his aunt shaking him. 'I know you've taken it!' she was crying. 'You've stolen my gold chain!' Bessy stood in the doorway of the bedroom watching the scene and growling softly.

William managed to say, 'I haven't stolen it.'

Of course, she did not believe him. She turned out all the pockets of his clothes. She unpacked his suitcase all over the floor. She took the mattress and all the bedding off the bedstead and searched them. She searched everywhere; and all the time she ranted at him and cuffed him and slapped him.

It was all no more than William had expected, but it was hard to bear. Doggedly he repeated, 'I haven't stolen it.'

He was late for school, of course; and he had to deliver a letter from his aunt to the headmaster. Later, the headmaster summoned him. 'William, do you know what was in the letter from your aunt?'

'About me?' said William. 'I can guess.'

The headmaster sighed. He said, 'I have written a note in reply to your aunt. I have suggested a time when she can call on me to discuss – things. William, you must be sure to deliver this note to your aunt; she is expecting to hear from me . . .'

The other boys were curious about William's interview with the headmaster. He told them nothing. The witty boy suggested that the head had noticed feathers beginning to sprout on Henny-penny's legs. This boy found two sparrow feathers in the playground and stuck them in William's hair when he was not looking.

At the end of the school day, William took the headmaster's note with him back to Aunt Rosa's house; but Aunt Rosa was out. There was a message for him on the kitchen table saying that there was no tea for him today, and that she would be back during the evening.

He did not mind about the food; but – later – he did mind about not being able to get into his bedroom. Bessy lay along the threshold, watching him and growling. She would not let him pass. He said aloud, 'You don't want me here; but I don't want to be here. So we're quits.' That made him feel better about Bessy.

He took the headmaster's note from his pocket, put it on the floor and pushed it with his foot towards Bessy. She seized it angrily in her teeth and tore it into shreds.

He went downstairs and into the garden, to the bottom of it. All the hens were out in the orchard, and he could see the cockerel among them. He went to the hen-house, opened the door, and looked in. The fresh straw smelled pleasantly; and there was his dear nest egg . . .

He stooped and crept inside the hen-house, and pulled the door after him as closely shut as possible. He fumbled in the straw for the nest egg and found it, and shook it gently, to hear the comforting sound of the chain moving inside.

He settled in the fresh straw on the far side of the

hen-house from the roosting perch. At first he sat there; then, beginning to feel drowsy, he lay down in the straw. He fell asleep with the nest egg up to his cheek.

He slept deeply, dreamlessly, and better than he had ever slept in Aunt Rosa's house.

So he never noticed the fading of daylight, and the hens and cockerel that came stooping in through their pop-hole, into the hen-house for the night. They saw William there, and were disturbed at the sight; but he made no movement or sound, and they reassured themselves. One by one they flew up on the perch, and roosted there, and slept.

He never heard later the voice of his Aunt Rosa calling distractedly up and down the garden and in the orchard, as she had already done inside the house. Neighbours were consulted and gave advice; at last the police were summoned; there was a great deal of telephoning. William slept through it all, his nest egg to his face.

With the first of daylight the hens and cockerel left the hen-house for the run, and then – since no one had thought of shutting them up last night – for the orchard. The cockerel often stopped to crow; but William did not hear him. He slept on.

The sun was high in the sky before William woke. At first he did not remember where he was. In his own old room at home? In Aunt Rosa's cold house? Neither. He was in a *hen-house*: he had slept there, the whole night through, with the hens and with his old enemy, the cockerel. He laughed aloud. He felt light-hearted, as he had not done for many weeks. He also felt very hungry.

The hens and cockerel had gone; it was time for him to go, too. He did not know what was going to happen next; but at least he had had a long night's sleep in freedom; and he had his precious nest egg safe in his pocket.

He let himself out of the hen-house. He began walking up the garden path towards the house – towards Aunt Rosa's house. As he came nearer, his spirits sank lower: he was walking towards a prison.

Aunt Rosa would be waiting for him. And there she was – a figure standing on the garden doorstep; and – but no! it was not his Aunt Rosa. It was his father.

With a wild cry William ran into his father's arms, and his father picked him up and hugged him safe. 'William! William!' he repeated, over and over again.

It was some time before any scolding began: 'Why on earth did you run away? You bad boy – you silly boy! Where did you go! Your aunt was out of her mind with worry, so she telephoned me and I drove all through the night to come. William, you should never, never have run away like that!'

'But I didn't run away,' said William. 'I was here all the time.'

'Where?'

'Just in the hen-house at the bottom of the garden.'

William's father began to laugh. 'And you've straw all over your clothes!'

He took his son indoors to Aunt Rosa – Aunt Rosa, sleep-starved, haggard with many fears, and by now, fortunately, speechless with fatigue. He explained that William was back. ('But I've never been away,' protested William. 'The hen-house isn't away.')

William's father said that, now he was here, he might as well take William off Aunt Rosa's hands. She nodded. It wasn't that he wasn't grateful to her – Aunt Rosa nodded again – but he needed his son to be with him, after all. William was all he had now. 'And somehow we'll manage,' said William's father. 'I'm not sure how, but we shall manage.'

Then Aunt Rosa said she was going to bed; and she went, with Bessy following her. Bessy had had an extraordinarily disagreeable night, with upsets and unwanted visitors.

William's father telephoned the police and told the neighbours about William's return. Then he took over Aunt Rosa's kitchen and made an enormous breakfast for himself and William. After that, they packed everything into William's suitcase, got into the car, and drove off. They did not wake Aunt Rosa to say goodbye, but William's father left a note on the kitchen table.

When the car had taken them well away from Aunt Rosa's house, William said, 'I liked her hen-house and her hens.'

His father said, 'But Rosa said you were frightened of the cockerel.'

'I was afraid of him,' said William, 'but I liked him, too. He was only fierce when he was defending his hens, his family.'

His father glanced down at something William had just taken out of his pocket. 'Did Rosa give you that dummy egg?'

'No,' said William. 'I took it.'

His father frowned. 'That's stealing.'

'I just *needed* it.'

'It's still stealing. You'll have to send it back.'

'It might break in the post. Couldn't we send the money instead?' William had a brilliant idea. 'You could stop it out of my pocket money, and you could tell Aunt Rosa that. That would really please her.'

So it was settled. But, after a while, hesitantly, William asked, 'Did Aunt Rosa ever say I'd stolen anything?'

'No,' his father said, quite positively. 'But then, she didn't know about this egg, did she?'

William thought: she'd tell the headmaster, but she wouldn't dare tell my dad about the chain. Because he knew it was my mum's, and I'd given it to my mum. I wasn't stealing. I just took back.

He tilted the egg in his hands, to feel the movement inside it. He said, 'I shall always keep this egg. On my mantelpiece.'

'You do that,' said his father. 'Only we shall have to

find somewhere to live with a room with a mantel-piece in it.'

'We'll manage somehow,' William said comfortably. 'You said so.'

# Inside Her Head

It was a hot, hot afternoon, and for once Elm Street was empty of children. A good many of the Elm Street lot had gone away on summer holidays; the rest had gone round the corner to the Lido to splash and swim and eat ice-cream with their toes in the water. Except for one.

Except for Sim Tolland.

Sim Tolland was at home having chicken-pox. He lay in bed with the window down as far as possible: the heavy, still air lay – so he thought – like an enormous plank balanced across the top sash. Only a sheet covered his sweaty, spotty body. He felt awful. The chicken-pox made him feel awful, and the heat of the

108

bedroom – which was the heat of the bedroom plus the heat of the downstairs rooms which had risen to join it – also made him feel awful. And he felt particularly awful when he thought of the others at the Lido or by the sea or in a cool, green countryside.

His mother poked her head round the bedroom door, gave a quick glance to check that his lemonade jug was full, and said, 'Mrs Crackenthorpe to see you.' She went away again.

Old Mrs Crackenthorpe, from the other end of Elm Street, was known to have a soft spot for Sim Tolland. Sim groaned. This was even more awful than awful.

He heard the slow heavy tread on the stairs, the little gasps of effort. Mrs Crackenthorpe eased herself into the room and on to a chair. She perspired gently.

'I've had chicken-pox, dear,' she said. She took something from a brown-paper bag. 'Jelly babies to cheer you up. You *need* jelly babies.'

'Thanks,' said Sim. 'But just now I couldn't . . .'

'It's the heat, dear.'

'Yes,' said Sim.

'And the chicken-pox.'

'Yes,' said Sim.

They fell silent, while Mrs Crackenthorpe tried carefully to think of some other way of cheering up Sim Tolland. At last she said, 'I didn't bring any comics or anything for you to look at. I thought you wouldn't want to read.'

'I don't,' said Sim, and then added quickly, 'And

I don't want to watch any more telly. Or listen to things.'

Mrs Crackenthorpe was still following her own train of thought. 'I didn't want to read, either. When I had chicken-pox. And it was very hot weather, too, just like now. Here, in Elm Street.'

It was, after all, unexpectedly soothing to listen to old Mrs Crackenthorpe rabbiting on.

'Nobody much ever came to see me,' Mrs Cracken-thorpe was saying sadly, 'because of the chicken-pox. It was dull. I was an only child – just about your age, or younger; and I'd never really had friends, anyway.' (Sim thought of *his* friends, all the Elm Street lot, coolly enjoying themselves elsewhere: he could have wept.) 'I didn't have friends because my mother liked to keep herself to herself. You know. She was very particular about me. So it was dull for me that summer.'

In the silence that followed, Sim could see that Mrs Crackenthorpe was pondering something difficult. She came to a decision. She began: 'When you're in bed, you think a lot.' She tapped the side of her head just above her ear. 'Inside your head. I mean, *right* inside your head. Oh, you'd be surprised!'

'Yes?' said Sim.

'In the middle of the night, when you can't sleep for the heat and the chicken-pox, and it's so dull . . .'

'Go on,' said Sim.

'Well, to begin with, there was the elm tree –'

'The elm tree stump,' corrected Sim. It was well

known in the Street as the meeting place for the Elm Street lot – always had been. It had always been there: a stump.

But Mrs Crackenthorpe was surprisingly firm. 'A tree,' she said. 'In those days, when I was a child in Elm Street, it was a tree – not a cut-down stump. A tree, taller than the houses, reaching from side to side of the street. Green leaves. When there wasn't a breath of wind anywhere else, there was always a breath up among those leaves. The leaves –' She searched for a word. 'The leaves *rustled*. It sounded cool up there, where the leaves rustled. So I thought.'

Sim thought of green leaves and cool breezes. Greenness; coolness . . . 'Yes . . .'

'So one night I decided to go up there.'

'You *what*?'

'Decided to climb up there,' said Mrs Cracken-thorpe. 'And I did.'

'Decided or climbed?'

'Both.'

There was a disbelieving silence from Sim's bed.

'I was a little girl then,' said Mrs Crackenthorpe. 'Plump, of course, but light, small, neat. Do you know, I'd never even thought of climbing a tree before?'

This was another extraordinary thing for Sim to have to believe.

'My mother always liked me to keep my clothes clean, you see. She insisted. But that particular night they'd gone to bed, and I lay awake, too hot and

111

chicken-poxy to sleep. I could see the elm tree from my window. I could see the leaves at the top moving in the breeze that was always there. The moon shone through the leaves. Bright moonlight, or I don't think I'd have dared . . .'

'Dared . . .' repeated Sim Tolland. He looked at Mrs Crackenthorpe sitting there, overflowing the bedroom chair; then he closed his eyes for a moment to try to imagine her a plump, small, neat little girl, *daring* . . .

'Just in my nightie,' said Mrs Crackenthorpe. 'Not even bedroom slippers. I went downstairs and into the street, all moonlit, and to the tree and up it —'

'How "up it"?' interrupted Sim. 'A tree like that doesn't have branches near the ground. They start high up — too high for you to reach, if you were a little girl.'

'Let me think, then,' said Mrs Crackenthorpe. 'A ladder?'

'No,' said Sim. 'You couldn't have lugged a ladder out. Not if you were just a little girl.'

'You're right, of course,' said Mrs Crackenthorpe, dashed. Then she brightened: 'How about this, then? There happened to be one of those very tall vans with a sort of roof-rack and sort of rungs up the side of the van to the roof-rack — you know! And this van — well, it happened to be parked just under the elm tree.'

'Well . . .' said Sim.

'A real bit of luck for me, that van,' said Mrs Crackenthorpe, over-riding any possible objection or doubt from Sim. 'So I just climbed up the side of this van to its roof. From there I could easily reach the lowest branch of the tree, and climb on to it. Then up and up, from branch to branch. I turned out to be a natural climber. From branch to branch,' Mrs Crackenthorpe repeated dreamily, 'up and up, breezier and breezier, cooler and cooler . . .' She was fanning herself deliciously with the brown-paper bag from which she had taken the packet of jelly babies.

She stopped suddenly, as a thought occurred to her: 'Oh dear! Do you think I ought to have taken a cushion with me?'

'Whatever for?' said Sim.

'To sit on, of course. The branches would have been uncomfortable without a cushion. So I did take a cushion. And do you know how high I climbed with that cushion?'

'No. How high?'

'To the top. To the very top. I wasn't afraid – not one bit. I climbed to where the branches grew quite thin and whippy. I settled that cushion in the elbow of a branch and I settled myself on it, and I was comfortable and cool – so cool. All night long I stayed there. Do you think I might even have dozed off up there? I wasn't a bit afraid, you know.'

'No,' said Sim. 'Too risky. You might have fallen.'

Mrs Crackenthorpe was only a little disappointed. 'Oh, well . . . So I stayed awake all night, but cool and comfortable. I suppose I saw the dawn from that tree-top.' She sighed. 'Oh, the dawn was so beautiful . . .'

'What happened when your mother . . .?'

'Let's see. Yes, I think they all came rushing out of the house. They shouted and cried and tried to get me to come down. But I was like a cat caught up a tree: I'd gone too high. My dad came up the tree after me, but he was a big, heavy man – it runs in the family. He got scared when he got really high and the branches began to be thin and whippy, as I've said. So he climbed down again.'

'And did no one else try?'

'All the neighbours had come out by then, and were calling up the tree to me. So – let's see . . . Yes, some young fellow thinner than my dad came climbing up the tree, but even he daren't come right to the top, where I was. All he could do was reach up and tickle the sole of my foot. I shrieked, and everyone shouted to him to leave me alone and come down again. So he did.'

'I like that bit,' said Sim.

Mrs Crackenthorpe smiled and bobbed her head in acknowledgement, and went on. 'Then my mother fetched all the blankets out of the house and made everybody hold the corners of them, drawn taut, all round the tree, close in. In case I fell. And they waited . . .'

'Did you fall?'

'Of course not.'

'Then how on earth *did* you get down?'

'There was a clanging and a rushing up,' said

114

Mrs Crackenthorpe, 'and they'd sent for the fire-brigade.'

Sim couldn't help being impressed: 'I say!'

'The first I knew of it was one of those shiny brass helmets coming up through the leaves at the top of the tree.'

'You hadn't seen the firemen below, on the ground?'

'No,' said Mrs Crackenthorpe. Then, anxiously: 'Why?'

'Well, how come you could see the people with the blankets, if you couldn't see the firemen?'

'Oh, dear!' said Mrs Crackenthorpe, taken aback. Then she pulled herself together: 'I just *couldn't*. The leaves must have shifted in the breeze, I suppose. Anyway, as I've told you: there was this fireman's helmet coming through the leaves at me. The fireman was on one of those special ladders they have that go straight up into the air. You know.' Mrs Crackenthorpe waved a hand vaguely.

'Go on.'

'He called to me, all jolly, as if I were a cat caught up there. "Kitty! Kitty! Kitty!" he called. I let him help me off my branch, and he carried me down the ladder to the bottom.'

'What about the cushion?'

'That fell.'

'You could have carried it down, if you carried it up.'

'Have it your own way,' said Mrs Crackenthorpe. 'I carried it down.'

There was a long pause.

'That's the end of the story,' said Mrs Crackenthorpe.

'Not a story,' said Sim. 'It happened. You said.'

'Oh, yes,' said Mrs Crackenthorpe. 'Yes, yes, yes!'

'It was true,' said Sim.

'It happened,' said Mrs Crackenthorpe.

'But there's no proof,' said Sim, suddenly discontented.

'Well,' said Mrs Crackenthorpe slowly, 'what about this? Ever after that, people have called me Kitty, as a joke. They still do. Kitty Crackenthorpe.'

'Everybody?'

'Yes.'

'Mr Crackenthorpe calls you Kitty, too?'

Mrs Crackenthorpe flinched, but, 'Yes,' she said.

Exactly at that moment Sim's mother called from downstairs: 'Mrs Crackenthorpe, Mr Crackenthorpe's here asking if you're coming home to tea.'

'Oh, yes, yes, yes!' cried Mrs Crackenthorpe, gathering her flesh together, flustered. All Elm Street knew that Mr Crackenthorpe was not a good-tempered man.

'Are you coming, then?' shouted Mr Crackenthorpe from below.

'Oh, yes, yes, yes!' gasped Mrs Crackenthorpe, now up from her chair and waddling towards the bedroom door.

'Elsie, do you hear me?'

'*Elsie* . . .' said Sim reproachfully. 'But you definitely said –'

From the doorway Mrs Crackenthorpe spoke hurriedly over her shoulder: 'Lying in bed, you can think a lot of things. Inside your head. You can make things *happen* inside your head. Happenings. Real adventures . . .' She was gasping for words and for breath.

From below: 'ELSIE!'

Mrs Crackenthorpe's last wheezy whispers reached Sim from just outside his bedroom door: 'You shut your eyes, Sim Tolland. You try it. Remember: inside your head.' Then a slow thumping down the stairs and Mrs Crackenthorpe was gone.

Thoughtfully Sim collected the packet of jelly babies from the sheet where Mrs Crackenthorpe had dropped it. He broke it open and popped a jelly baby into his mouth. But no, he'd lost his taste for jelly babies.

He spat the baby out on to a saucer by his bedside that already held some grape pips.

He was still thinking of what Mrs Crackenthorpe had told him. She had climbed a tree. Well, he was pretty sure he could think of an even better, cooler thing to happen. Inside his head.

He settled himself as comfortably as possible. Then he shut his eyes.

Choosing a brilliant book
can be a tricky business...
but not any more

# www.puffin.co.uk

**The best selection of books at your fingertips**

## So get clicking!

# Read more in Puffin

For complete information about books available from Puffin – and Penguin – and how to order them, contact us at the appropriate address below. Please note that for copyright reasons the selection of books varies from country to country.

# www.puffin.co.uk

In the United Kingdom: Please write to Dept EP, Penguin Books Ltd, Bath Road, Harmondsworth, West Drayton, Middlesex UB7 ODA

In the United States: Please write to Penguin Putnam Inc., P.O. Box 12289, Dept B, Newark, New Jersey 07101–5289 or call 1–800–788–6262

In Canada: Please write to Penguin Books Canada Ltd, 10 Alcorn Avenue, Suite 300, Toronto, Ontario M4V 3B2

In Australia: Please write to Penguin Books Australia Ltd, P.O. Box 257, Ringwood, Victoria 3134

In New Zealand: Please write to Penguin Books (NZ) Ltd, Private Bag 102902, North Shore Mail Centre, Auckland 10

In India: Please write to Penguin Books India Pvt Ltd, 11 Panscheel Shopping Centre, Panscheel Park, New Delhi 110 017

In the Netherlands: Please write to Penguin Books Netherlands bv, Postbus 3507, NL–1001 AH Amsterdam

In Germany: Please write to Penguin Books Deutschland GmbH, Metzlerstrasse 26, 60594 Frankfurt am Main

In Spain: Please write to Penguin Books S. A., Bravo Murillo 19, 1° B, 28015 Madrid

In Italy: Please write to Penguin Italia s.r.l., Via Felice Casati 20, I–20124 Milano

In France: Please write to Penguin France S. A., 17 rue Lejeune, F–31000 Toulouse

In Japan: Please write to Penguin Books Japan, Ishikiribashi Building, 2–5–4, Suido, Bunkyo-ku, Tokyo 112

In South Africa: Please write to Longman Penguin Southern Africa (Pty) Ltd, Private Bag X08, Bertsham 2013